TEXAS COWBOY'S HONOR

BARB HAN

TORJAKE PUBLISHING

Editing: Ali Williams

Cover Design: Jacob's Cover Designs

For my family. I'm so fortunate to get to do life with each of you. My love for you has no bounds and I count my blessings every day.

1

Savannah Moore walked into her apartment, kicked off her heels and tossed her keys onto the side table. She'd been thinking about getting those shoes off for the past two hours. The walk from her car had felt like stepping on nails.

"That's so much better." She picked up the pumps, thinking if she had many more days like this one she'd start wearing tennis shoes to work. And she definitely should've worn a fitness tracking device instead of her wristwatch. At least then she'd be able to count her steps and get credit for taking the stairs instead of the elevator.

Jenny Dixon, her roommate, looked up at Savannah from over the top of the popcorn bowl on her lap. She sat cross-legged on the couch with two textbooks splayed out on one side and her spiral notebooks stacked and opened to her right. Her laptop sat on the floor in front of her. The pen tucked above her right ear and ink stains on her fingers were good indicators that she'd been working for hours.

"Long day?"

"Since when is a twelve-hour work day *long*?" She drew out the last word. It was long-past dark on what had been a cloudy April day. Tree allergies were hitting record levels in Texas this time of year and the humidity had held all of the gunk close to the earth. Savannah felt every bit of it in her sinuses. Walking from the A/C in her building into the balmy night air had drenched her new silk blouse in a matter of seconds.

The sarcasm wasn't lost on Jenny based on her pinched expression. She rolled her eyes. "That's the fifth time in five consecutive days. When did Alvin and Tate become an accounting sweatshop?"

"I've been strongly encouraged not to make it 'look like' I'm working as hard as I am."

"What does that even mean?"

"Mr. Alvin wants me to cut down on my billable hours to my clients and basically 'volunteer' some of my time to the company."

"That sounds wrong on so many levels."

Savannah wouldn't disagree there. "He also doesn't seem to think I need a personal life." Not that hers was in peak form as of late but constantly being at work wasn't helping resuscitate a dead dating life.

"You could always quit the firm." Jenny batted her eyelashes at Savannah.

"I know you're kidding but I'm so tempted to do just that right now."

"My boss was totally checking you out the other day when you dropped my apron off for me at lunch. I'm sure he'd hire you and then we could be co-workers. You could work at B-B-Q like me." Jenny laughed.

"And blow my first real promotion on my first real job?" Savannah pinched her index finger and thumb together. "I'm this close to the corner office."

Now, they both laughed.

"Come on. The waitressing world needs good people like you." Jenny made a show of pouting. Then, she cracked up at herself. She seemed like she'd been at the books too long.

"Technically, you're a graduate student. And I can tell you've been on that couch a while when you start making corny jokes and actually laughing at them." Jenny's education was funded by her parents, but Savannah knew her roommate worked hard at her studies and kept a part-time job because she liked the idea of making her own money. Savannah's only living relative, her aunt, lived a couple hours away in Gunner. Her own parents died in a boating accident her senior year of high school. Speaking of Aunt Becky, Savannah owed her an e-mail. She missed their monthly chats since she'd started working full-time. They were lucky to talk a few times a year now.

"*Technically*, I have to keep studying right now or I won't be a grad student much longer." Jenny motioned toward the opened books and then the notebook next to her on the brown leather couch.

The volume on the TV was low. Jenny had a habit of keeping a little background noise on when she was home and it especially seemed to help when she studied.

"All I want is food and sleep, and not necessarily in that order." Savannah questioned whether or not the other half of her peanut butter and jelly sandwich that she'd eaten four hours ago would hold until morning. Her stomach growled in answer, so she moved into the kitchen and straight to the fridge.

There was Greek yogurt, an apple, and an almost-empty milk carton.

"Was it my turn to go grocery shopping?" For someone who excelled with numbers, she wasn't very good at estimating how many days a gallon of milk would last two people. She groaned at the nearly-bare shelves.

"Afraid so."

"Figures. Sorry about that." Thankfully, Jenny was one of the least high maintenance people Savannah had ever known. But now, her already non-exciting Saturday of sleeping until noon, cleaning her room and then doing laundry just got a whole lot more boring. Grocery shopping was her least favorite chore and that was most likely the reason she put it off until the cupboards were just sad.

Her current life, dull as it might be, was still better than going out with Toby.

"It's fine. I had cereal." Jenny waved a hand in the air, her black hair swishing in its messy bun.

Savannah perked up as she moved toward the cabinet. "Any left?"

"No. Got the last bowl."

That shouldn't make Savannah as sad as it did. Her exhaustion was finally catching up with her and that tended to make her emotions dramatic. "What do you want for breakfast tomorrow, the apple or the yogurt?"

"You pick."

Savannah settled on the yogurt. Vanilla. Her favorite.

"Don't stay up too late studying." Her warning was met with two thumbs up from Jenny.

Savannah knew her roommate would end up falling asleep on the couch, and wake with a horrible crick in her neck the next morning. After seven months of living together, and two years of friendship before that, Savannah knew the drill.

Fifteen minutes after washing her face and polishing off the yogurt, Savannah had her eyes closed and the lights out. She had no idea how long she'd been asleep when she heard the first scream.

Savannah sat bolt upright. The noise in the next room was loud. She didn't want her neighbors complaining about the TV again.

A crash sounded in the adjacent room. She rubbed blurry eyes. Hold on. *That* couldn't have been the TV. She grabbed her cell from the nightstand next to her bed. The battery was low. She could only pray there was enough juice left if it came down to needing to use it.

Another scream, muffled this time, caused icy fingers to grip her spine. The noise couldn't possibly be the television. She listened closer. It had been too real to be some lame pop-up ad on Jenny's laptop. That had happened once, horrifying them both.

Someone was in the apartment.

On her tiptoes, Savannah's breath caught in her throat as she neared her bedroom door. From where she stood, she was almost certain she heard Jenny crying as she hit three numbers on her phone's keypad. 911.

The phone to her ear, she whispered, "Someone is in my house."

"What's your name, ma'am?"

"Savannah" She rattled off her address before setting the phone down. She didn't have time to explain the situation. Jenny needed her.

Frantic, she moved to her closet and searched for some kind of weapon she could use against what had to be an intruder. Anything would do.

Rummaging around, her fingers curled around the grip of one of Toby's golf clubs. He'd left in a huff when she'd ended the relationship and hadn't come back for the few of his things he'd left behind. She never expected to be using the club like this when she'd shoved it deep in her closet in case he asked for it back.

Gripping the long metal rod as though it was a baseball bat, she moved quietly to the door.

Slowly, carefully, Savannah turned the door handle. She peeked out and saw her worst fear, Jenny's body being pressed against the wall.

From this vantage point, all Savannah could see of Jenny's attacker was that he was the size of a linebacker. He wore a hoodie, and she was suddenly struck by the fact that that was the only thing she'd be able to describe; no hair color, no facial features, nothing.

Linebacker shifted slightly to his right, just enough for Savannah to see Jenny's face clearly. Her cheeks were puffy and red. Her eyes rolled back in her head. She looked like she was about to pass out.

Savannah turned to pick up her cell phone and find out where the hell the cops were. Her shoulder banged against the bedroom door.

The attacker whirled around, no doubt following the noise. His gaze locked onto Savannah, who changed her plans on a dime and charged toward him, golf club raised.

Jenny's limp body dropped to the floor.

"The cops are on their way," Savannah shouted at the man racing toward her, angry tears blinding her. She twisted her body and then brought the golf club around, swinging with everything she had.

She stared into the blackest eyes for a split-second and then froze as the intruder caught the club with one hand. Midair, he yanked at the golf club. Savannah's entire body jolted to the right. The man was as strong as a tank.

His dead-looking eyes bore into her. Hers had adjusted to the dark, so she could see that his were brown. If she was five-feet-seven-inches, he was easily six-foot-three. His long hair was greasy and blacker than night. He grinned in a show of big, yellow horse-like teeth. Darkness emanated from him.

In that moment, she looked into the depths of pure hatred.

From her peripheral, she could see Jenny's lifeless body in a crumple on the floor and panic rippled through her.

In the next second, the intruder backed Savannah up enough steps to slam the back of her head against the wall. The ringing noise in her ears was deafening as she scratched him with her nails, doing anything she possibly could to stop him from snapping her neck in two.

And that's exactly what he tried to do.

Using his right hand, he gripped her neck and squeezed. She gasped for air. Her lungs seized, and her throat burned.

Screaming would do no good. Actually, attempting to scream would do no good. There was no way she could get enough air to manage a good scream.

Using both of her hands, Savannah clawed at the vise-like grips around her neck. She was getting lightheaded and figured it would only be a matter of seconds until she passed out. After, he would be able to do anything he wanted to her and Jenny. She couldn't let that happen.

Gathering all the strength she had left, she curled her legs up. Planting her feet against Linebacker's stomach, she bucked, using her back against the wall as leverage.

Linebacker barely moved. His nose was mere inches from hers. In that moment, she feared his face would be the last thing she ever saw.

And then she heard it. A strong male voice sounded from the living room. Her salvation.

"Put your hands where I can see them." There was no doubt the stern-sounding officer meant business.

Savannah saw stars. Her vision blurred. She was about to black out.

"Hands in the air." The officer's high-pitched command broke through the whoosh sound in her ears.

Consciousness was slipping out of her grasp. Just when she was about to give in, Linebacker's face twisted into a grimace.

"This is not the last time you'll see me." His vow was delivered through clenched teeth.

Suddenly, the vise-like grip around her throat released and she slid to the floor while Linebacker was being thrusted against the wall. Gasping, her lungs clawed for air while he was being handcuffed and an officer came running toward her.

Panicking, her gaze locked onto her roommate's lifeless body in the adjacent room where officers had started life-saving measures.

And in that moment, Savannah realized her life would never be the same again.

2

One year later...

Liam Quinn stared at the phone on his nightstand where he stayed at Gunner Inn. News that he was back in his home town would spread faster than wildfire and he relished these few last minutes of privacy. He'd arrived last night just before midnight, hoping to get a good night's sleep before he faced his family and Quinnland Ranch.

Lot of good that thinking had done. He'd tossed and turned for most of the few hours he'd actually stayed in bed. The others had been spent either getting a glass of water or pacing the floor while checking his phone.

Yeah, he was off his game. He'd swallowed enough water to float a barge last night and he'd never checked his e-mail more. Normally, he couldn't care less about his phone. Working on a ranch, cell coverage was always spotty; half the time he forgot he had the damn thing with him. The other half, he didn't care.

And yet, strangely, there was something right about being here in town that escaped explanation. He'd spent more than seven years living and working at a friend's ranch in Colorado, but Liam was surprised to find out how much being back in Texas felt like home.

Even though, a little voice in the back of his head decided to point out that he technically wasn't *home*.

Quinnland was the place he'd grown up with six brothers and five cousins. He and his brother Isaac were identical twins.

The clock on the nightstand next to the bed read six a.m. Work on the ranch had started a solid hour-and-a-half ago. Three of his brothers, including Isaac, now lived on and worked the ranch full-time.

Liam loved the outdoors and working cattle. The thought of going back to the place where he grew up, though, where he'd lost the other two most important people in his life? He couldn't go there in his mind.

No matter how many times he closed his eyes he ended up staring at the ceiling. Since repeating that and expecting sleep was as productive as trying to get honey from a wasp, Liam threw his legs over the side of the bed. His stomach growled, and he thought about the tiny sandwich he'd eaten for dinner that had been named Big Burger. The owners of that pit stop must've had one helluva sense of humor. But even more than food, he needed caffeine. An IV hookup was preferred but he'd take his coffee any way he could get it at this stage.

Liam walked into the bathroom, washed his face, and then brushed his teeth. The bakery next door to the Inn would be his first stop. After that, he'd consider making a trip to Quinnland. Contact with his brothers could wait until after breakfast.

He threw on some clothes and tucked his feet into boots. A quick finger-comb through his hair and then finally he threw on his Stetson. Since this was as respectable as he'd get at this hour of the morning, Liam grabbed his wallet and phone before heading out the door. He took the steps quickly, reaching the bottom of the stairs in a matter of seconds.

Becky Stillwater used to own and run the bakery next door to the inn. He hoped she still did.

Once he saw the line, his hope was confirmed. The line for the small bakery was out the door. Liam took it as a good sign. A line the size of this one meant the food was still topnotch. Anything had to be better than that bite-sized burger he'd had for supper. Burger Bite. Now that would've made sense to him. He would've ordered half a dozen instead of one.

The smell of fresh baked bread hit him, causing his stomach to revolt. Impatience edged. He nodded to the male who was in line in front of him. The guy had been ogling Liam for a solid couple of minutes and he figured he was being confused for his brother. Isaac had moved back to Gunner a few short weeks ago.

The guy looked like he was working up to say something to Liam, so he turned to look the opposite direction. Talking would require caffeine that was not in his system yet. The smell of freshly baked goods along with dark roast coffee assaulted his senses once again. The degree of his hunger made itself known.

At least the line was moving quickly. He also noticed men outnumbered women in the line, which was more of an interesting side note than an earth-shattering discovery. Still, he took note. The cattle business boomed in Gunner this time of year and there were plenty of seasonal workers in town with more new faces than he cared to count. The faces might change but the cycles didn't and neither did the fixtures, like Ms. Becky's place.

Liam stared at the cell phone in his hand, thinking about the calls he needed to make. It wasn't that he didn't want to see or speak to his brothers. He loved every single one of them. They'd been close growing up and even though they'd gone their separate ways as adults, Liam never once doubted the fact they loved each other.

It was the baggage that came with them that Liam wished he could avoid. Their father, millionaire cattle rancher T.J. Quinn, had called Liam and his brothers home for some big announcement. Liam wouldn't have bothered to come on T.J.'s account, especially considering he'd never been close with his old man. It was Liam's twin who'd gotten through to him.

Plus, the fact Isaac had gotten married and adopted a little girl. Since Liam had been avoiding all messages from home for the past year, he'd missed his twin brother's wedding. That was a mistake on his part. One he needed to rectify.

He and his brothers had been especially close during childhood. No doubt a product of having grown up under T.J.'s iron-fisted rule. Liam's mother had suddenly died shortly after the birth of his youngest brother, Phoenix. If it hadn't been for their housekeeper and nanny, Marianne, Liam figured he and his brothers would've turned out a helluva lot differently. She'd been the saving grace of a childhood that had been run more like a military unit than a family. Up by four a.m. to work the ranch before school. No time for grieving. No patience for emotions. And a heavy hand from their father if he thought one of the boys got out of line.

Just thinking about T.J. caused Liam's shoulders to tense. Liam had no idea what the man wanted now. However, his brother had made a strong suggestion the news might have something to do with their father's health. The idea on the table was that maybe T.J. wouldn't be around much longer. No matter how bad the past had been, it was in the past. Liam didn't want his father to die without having the conversation they needed to have.

T.J. sick, though? Liam couldn't imagine it. Didn't men like T.J. live forever?

Those last two words sat bitterly in Liam's thoughts. A couple steps closer to the magic counter and his stomach growled again.

As he blinked up, a woman caught his gaze. She came from out of the back room, carrying a tray of something—he couldn't be sure what because he couldn't take his eyes off her. An unexpected jolt of electricity shot through him. Now, he was awake and wondering who the beauty behind the counter was.

She smiled at the customer ahead of him, but it didn't reach those beautiful amber eyes of hers. She was medium height and had just the right amount of curves to make his fingers itch to touch her. Silky hair fell way past her shoulders and had been pulled off her face in a ponytail.

Granted, he hadn't been back to Gunner a few years. The second looks he'd been getting while standing in line with accompanying head nods were proof folks were confusing him with Isaac. People came and went but the core of Gunner, Texas, rarely ever changed.

And Liam was damn certain he'd remember if he ever laid eyes on this woman before.

Clearly, he wasn't the only one who'd noticed. He almost laughed out loud when he realized the reason for the line had nothing to do with the smell of fresh bread and everything to do with the blonde serving it. Several men in the line straightened their shoulders the minute she looked up.

Someone behind Liam cleared his throat. Much to Liam's embarrassment, he realized the line had moved and he hadn't. Shaking his head, he took a couple of steps closer to the counter, but he couldn't tear his gaze away from the blonde-haired beauty standing a few feet away.

The man in front of Liam seemed to have the same issue and Liam figured most others were probably just as guilty. And since stalking wasn't his forte, he refocused on the menu above her head.

"Can I help you with something?" Her voice had a musical quality to it as she helped the gentleman in front of Liam. The guy gave his order.

Liam couldn't help but notice the way the blonde kept her arms folded across her chest while she listened. She kept enough distance from the case that no one could reach across it to touch her and there was a fearful quality to her eyes. The rest of her body language was just as defensive as she moved toward the register after giving the customer his order. Everything about her said she was closed off.

"Liam Quinn. Is that you?" Becky Stillwater's voice bubbled across the room.

Eyes darted toward him. For all his efforts to go incognito, he'd been caught.

"Yes, ma'am." Liam hadn't noticed Becky Stillwater standing there. He'd been too busy staring at the blonde. He was pretty certain Ms. Becky had just busted him. And that was just awkward as hell. So much for slipping in for a quick breakfast and a cup of coffee while staying under the radar.

"It can't be you," Ms. Becky argued.

"In the flesh. I'm afraid it is."

The blonde glanced up at him, their eyes locked for a split second and he took a shot to the heart.

She diverted her gaze almost as quickly. The slight flush to her creamy skin did not go unnoticed by Liam. But he wasn't there to meet someone, he already had a date with some sweet caffeine. Strong cup. Hell, IV. He didn't care which he just needed some damn coffee.

Ms. Becky came around the counter and threw her arms around his waist. "I just saw your brother the other day. I didn't realize he had a family." Those words shouldn't strike a nerve with Liam. He didn't begrudge his brother. Isaac deserved happiness. Liam couldn't help but think about his own loss no matter how much he tried to keep the focus on his brother. Ms. Becky didn't miss a beat and Liam was thankful his heavy thoughts were interrupted. "Does this mean you're moving back, too?"

"No, ma'am. This is just a quick visit." Liam didn't figure it was a good idea to detail out his family's business. Plus, if T.J. really was sick, which Liam still couldn't fathom, it wouldn't be good to blast the news to the town before the family was ready to make an announcement. And there would have to be a formal admission.

News had a way of traveling real fast in a small town like Gunner. Liam hadn't exactly expected to slip into town unnoticed but he wasn't quite ready to face everyone just yet.

"What can I get for you this morning, Liam? It's on the house." He'd known Ms. Becky for the better part of his life. She'd always been kind, warm and generous. It was good to see that some things didn't change no matter how much time passed.

"Those croissants look and smell amazing. Other than that, just black coffee. Strong. Big cup." A twinge of regret ran through him. He'd really been hoping to have a reason to speak to the blonde.

"Coming right up." Ms. Becky turned to her employee, who was ringing up her last customer at the register. "Savannah, I'd like you to meet Liam Quinn."

Recognition seemed to dawn. Her eyes widened just enough for him to know she recognized his last name. Most people did. The

Quinn family was one of the wealthiest cattle ranching families in Texas. It was a shock that Liam had been in line this long with only a few nods in his direction. But then it was early, there were lots of new faces and folks here for coffee to wake them up. And, he now realized, much of the line most likely showed to have a reason to talk to the blonde. Hadn't he seen Bobby Raider lurking around the front window?

Liam made a mental note to keep watch for Bobby. The guy had a reputation for locking onto new women in town, and not knowing when to leave well enough alone.

"Nice to meet you." Liam tipped his hat toward Savannah.

She glanced at him with a smile. Shy?

"My niece just moved to Gunner to be near me and help out with the family business. She's staying with me until she finds her own place."

Savannah returned her full focus to the cash register. The keys seemed pretty damn interesting to her. And he noticed her cheeks seemed to flame. Was she uncomfortable being introduced around? Embarrassed that she lived with her aunt?

Liam couldn't get a good read on the beauty and that was most likely the reason he was drawn to her. She was new in town, a puzzle.

Or, maybe it was something else.

The flash of emotion behind her eyes that he couldn't quite put his finger on stirred his protective instincts. Both times she'd looked at him, she quickly returned her gaze to whatever she'd been doing before. Like he was a flame and if she stared directly at him for too long she'd catch fire.

Then again, it had been a long drive to Texas last night. He'd made the drive straight through without stopping for much more than coffee, the infamous tiny-tot-sized burger and the occasional bathroom break. Then there was the glorified nap he'd had last night instead of real sleep. All those factors combined probably had his mind playing tricks on him.

"How've you been, Ms. Becky?"

A pan clanked against the tile floor. Savannah covered her gasp with both hands and jumped away from the counter so fast he would've thought someone had just pulled a gun on her.

Her gaze darted around, searching for the source. Panic radiated from her in waves.

Much like a frightened animal, it damn sure looked like she was about to bolt.

~

A BURST of adrenaline shot through Savannah, her heart thundering in her chest so loud she could hear it in her ears.

"You're okay," Aunt Becky soothed but Savannah's fight, freeze or flight instincts had already kicked in. She'd mentally gone to that place in her mind where her roommate, Jenny, lay crumpled on the floor in the living room, victim to a vicious and deadly criminal. Those black eyes of Linebacker's were suddenly staring into Savannah's again. His angry fist clenched around her neck.

Savannah turned and ran toward the backroom. The nightmares were bad enough but any reminder during the day, any slight unexpected noise, caused a level of panic that made it almost impossible to function. The air felt like it had been stripped from the room and she struggled to breathe.

Frustration seethed as she pushed open the bathroom door. Seven months of Hapkido lessons after the home invasion in Austin and she still panicked and ran when her instincts kicked in. Wasn't that great?

From somewhere in the background, she heard her aunt's concerned voice.

Aunt Becky had a heart of gold and the best of intentions, so running into the bathroom like that felt like letting her down. Savannah gripped the sides of the porcelain sink as a tidal wave of anger roared through her, churning her insides like white foam pounding against the unforgiving sand.

The act of taking in air, breathing, burned her lungs.

She seriously needed a minute before returning to a room full of curious customers. Embarrassment would set in at some point later. Right now, she was just too frustrated and too pissed at herself to deal.

A splash of cold water on her face did little to wash away the panic attack gripping her lungs, making it almost impossible to breathe. Her thoughts immediately snapped to Jenny, and her heart broke all over again as a thin sheen of sweat broke out on her forehead.

Linebacker's real name was Harley Patterson. Reminding herself that he was a real person and not some superhuman devil usually helped calm her racing pulse.

Damn that bastard for taking away her friend. Damn him for taking away her sense of security. Damn him for taking away her home.

The city of Austin would never feel safe to her again. And after five moves in ten months, she'd decided to settle in Gunner with her only living relative. Even now, she couldn't be in a room with an unexpected noise without bolting first, asking questions later.

A soft knock at the door, a concerned voice that she recognized as Aunt Becky's, and another splash of cold water brought Savannah's stress response back to an almost reasonable level. She took in another deep breath before pulling herself together enough to face her kind relative.

Savannah cracked the door open. "I'm okay."

"It's really okay if you're not." Aunt Becky's voice was laced with compassion. Compassion that Savannah held onto like a life raft out to sea in a raging storm.

"I will be." At least, Savannah hoped she would be at some point. Definitely not today. Probably not tomorrow. But someday soon.

"Take your time. I can cover for you at the counter."

"Thank you, Aunt Becky."

Her aunt had taken a big risk on her by bringing her to Gunner, opening her home to Savannah and giving her a job at the bakery. She couldn't repay the kindness by hiding in the bathroom.

Savannah balled her fist, gathered her courage and straightened her apron. Another round of deep breaths later, and she stepped out of the bathroom.

Liam stood to the left of the register, his intense gaze focused on the swinging door to the back room. Coffee mug in hand, the concern lines etched in his forehead relaxed a notch when she returned to the counter.

"Sorry."

"Don't be." His deep timbre washed over her, causing a reaction that was wholly inappropriate under the circumstances.

The brief eye contact she made with Liam sent a jolt of electricity skittering across her skin. She'd had the same reaction to him a few minutes ago and didn't know what to do with it. She could count on one hand the number of dates she'd had in the past year. The few she'd been on had been attempts to move on from the nightmare. All had been abandoned with the sincerest of apologies.

On the last date, she'd made it all the way to the restaurant. Driving herself and meeting Benjamin there had been her one requirement for accepting the date. The thought of being alone in a car with a man she didn't know well enough to invite to Sunday supper with her parents when they'd been alive, usually caused her flight instinct to kick in.

She'd warned Benjamin well in advance that she doubted she was ready to date but blamed it on a bad breakup. He'd insisted. Said it was no big deal if she couldn't go through with the dinner.

She'd sat in her car for twenty-six minutes before the panic attack forced her to call the whole thing off.

With Carter, she'd made it to dessert before the red rash had crawled up her neck. The feeling like she was suffocating had almost overwhelmed her. She'd never eaten a piece of chocolate cake so fast in her life. Carter had seemed almost relieved.

After pitching in to pay the tab, her insistence, she'd gotten out of there and into her car in time for the true panic attack to hit.

Those were brutal. All the reminders to breathe in the world couldn't stave off the terror tightening in her chest.

Savannah reminded herself of all the things the counselor had said during their last few meetings. *Acknowledge. Accept. Accelerate.*

She'd just had a panic attack. There. She'd acknowledged it. This was a *feeling* and not something real. Her body was simply reacting to her mind freaking out. There. She'd accepted it. Now, it was time to accelerate the healing.

Deep breaths. Reminders she'd be okay.

And since none of those worked, she stepped a little closer to the cowboy she'd just met and handed over his order.

"Thank you." Liam was six-feet-four-inches of solid muscle. A warmth radiated from him, like he was the sun and all she had to do was stand near him to calm down.

"You're welcome."

Dark curls peeked out from underneath his Stetson, and he had the kind of chiseled features and strong jawline that could grace magazine covers. Damned if he wouldn't sell the entire stack. Standing with his legs apart in an athletic stance, he also looked like he could handle himself in pretty much any situation. So, it was probably nothing more than biology drawing her toward his light.

He moved to a table by the window and faced the door, giving her a birds-eye view of his profile. In that moment, she tried to convince herself that primal instinct was the only reason she'd noticed his strength. She was in panic mode and, therefore, drawn to the nearest male who looked like he could protect her.

How was that for awesome? Ten months of counseling and seven months of martial arts training couldn't stop biology from forcing her to search for a protector rather than looking to depend on herself.

She mentally rolled her eyes and took inventory of her situation. The last panic attack had sent her home for two days. The fact that she didn't feel the need to take the rest of the day off was progress. It wasn't much but she was gaining ground on her demons and that was something. Baby steps.

The morning rush kept Savannah busy enough to avoid eye contact with Liam for the next half hour. From his seat, he'd seemed intent on reading a newspaper that had been left on the table by its previous occupant. A few people had approached him at different times and he seemed cordial but uncomfortable with the attention. Boy, could she relate.

Now that the line had disappeared, she had time to clean tables. She started at the opposite side of the room. There were a dozen tables and a long breakfast bar pushed up against the front window that ran the length.

The closer she got to Liam, the quicker her pulse beat. This was different than the now-normal panic-attack rhythm. This was a feeling that had been taken from her along with so much else...this was attraction.

And she had no idea what to do with it.

3

"How long have you been in Gunner?"

One table at a time, Liam saw Savannah inching closer to him. He chalked up his attempt to start a conversation to the fact that he was avoiding those family phone calls he needed to make. A few folks had stopped by his table to welcome him back to Texas and ask how he was doing, no one seemed suspicious of the reason he was there. Whatever was going on with T.J. was being kept quiet.

"A little more than a month." She barely glanced up at him and when she did the frightened deer look returned. Her gaze bounced from the door that led to the kitchen to the one that led outside. He couldn't decide which path would win but he was curious as to why something like a dropped pan could cause the kind of stir it had for her.

Until her chin jutted out and she stared at him boldly. "Mind if I sit?"

He motioned toward the chair opposite him at the small round table. "Be my guest."

"I'm not originally from here." Her fingers worked the edges of the washrag in her hands after she took a seat. He didn't feel the need to point out the fact he'd have known if she was. Not only was she beautiful, memorable, but everyone knew each other in their tightknit community.

He studied her for a long moment. "Dallas?"

"Originally. But we moved to Austin when I was little. I stayed for college after my parents died in a boating accident toward the end of my senior year of high school. I'd already been accepted to University of Texas, so I stayed." There was a hint of sadness in her eyes when she spoke about her parents but mostly she was matter of fact, like someone who'd had more than a decade to come to terms with losing the people she'd loved.

Liam could only wonder if he'd ever get that same distance from the tragedy that had rocked him to the core and altered the course of his life. He pushed the thought aside, not wanting to focus on that right now.

"What brings you to Gunner?"

"My aunt asked me to help with the business." She broke eye contact and her cheeks flushed. She was a terrible liar.

Based on her reaction to the pan earlier, he figured she had her reasons. His mind automatically snapped to an abusive relationship and his grip tightened on the coffee mug in his hand. Liam lived by a code that said a real man never raised his hand to a woman or child. He reminded himself it was just a guess on his part.

When he didn't respond, Savannah turned the tables, "My aunt made it seem like this is a homecoming for you. What made you come back?"

"Family meeting."

"Your family name sounds really familiar." Recognition dawned in those beautiful amber eyes of hers. "You are one of the Quinns from Quinnland Ranch, aren't you?"

"That's right." Funny how he never thought of himself like that. It was interesting to see his life through a stranger's perspective. Living in Colorado for the past seven years had given him a fresh point of view. He no longer considered himself part of the family ranch business even though he would no doubt inherit Quinnland alongside his brothers at some point down the road.

Based on his brother's texts, *down the road* might come sooner than he thought.

"When did you get here?" Her delicate eyebrow arched just a bit and he wondered what that was about.

"Last night."

"I could've sworn I saw you in town a couple of days ago. You were far away, though, so I guess it could've been someone else."

"It was."

Now her brow really shot up.

"I have a twin brother by the name of Isaac. You aren't losing your mind. It was most likely him you saw."

That ah-ha moment settled across her face, like the world suddenly made sense. Liam told himself he had no business letting his gaze linger on that heart-shaped face, those full lips or her creamy skin. Her black irises were surrounded by the most beautiful shade of amber. She had the kind of eyes that made him think she could see right through him, and long shiny hair that made his fingers itch to get lost in the golden strands.

The feelings caught him off guard. He hadn't experienced anything of this magnitude in longer than he cared to remember and couldn't say he especially welcomed it now.

"That makes so much sense now." She worked the rag in her hands a little harder. Was that a nervous tick? He hoped he wasn't the reason because he was enjoying talking to her and hoped to do more of it while he was in town.

"You said you were here for a meeting. Does that mean you have no plans to stick around?"

"I have to get back to work. It's a busy time of year for cattle ranchers." He wouldn't be there now if his brothers hadn't impressed upon him the need to come home. After meeting Savannah, he owed them a thank you.

The door opened and Liam noticed that Bobby Raider slipped

inside the bakery, his gaze intent on Liam. He wondered if Savannah had picked up a new 'friend.'

Out of the corner of his eye, he saw Linda Decker approaching. The elderly widow stopped behind Savannah and cleared her throat.

Savannah nearly jumped out of her skin at the interruption. He half expected her to bolt to the back room again. Instead, she gripped his hand from across the table.

"Sorry." The mumbled apology wasn't necessary.

"It's okay." He did his level best to ignore the frisson of heat from contact. A hand touching his had never felt so intimate before. So, he stared at the spot for a second longer than he meant to after she'd let go.

"Can I help you with something, Mrs. Decker?" Savannah bolted to her feet and took a couple of steps backward, putting some distance between her and the widow.

"Would it be too much trouble to ask you to refill my mug?"

"Not at all." Savannah took the coffee cup from Mrs. Decker. She flashed her eyes at Liam before moving behind the counter and grabbing a carafe.

The widow followed, and Savannah handed the steaming mug over the counter where she seemed more comfortable interacting with others. Now, he was even more curious about what had happened to make her so uncomfortable with people.

Bobby Raider took the opportunity to slink up to the counter.

There was something wholly creepy about Bobby and always had been. At five-feet-nine-inches, he didn't have an imposing figure so that wasn't it. It was more the way he crept into a room, trying not to draw attention but watching everyone and everything. If the rumors from high school could be trusted, he'd been busted trying to peek into the girl's locker room more than once. Liam's hands fisted thinking about it. Bobby had been teased in middle school and Liam had always taken up for the underdog. But, if the rumors were true, Bobby didn't deserve anyone coming to his defense.

Savannah stayed behind the counter as a couple more customers trickled in. Liam tried to go back to reading the paper, but his mind was spinning and he felt compelled to keep one eye on Bobby. Questions swirled and he found that he wanted to know more about Gunner's newest resident.

Bobby shuffled his feet toward the counter and Liam kept the exchange in his peripheral. He couldn't hear their words over the buzz but he didn't like the way Bobby seemed unable to look Savannah in the eyes. He kept his head down and pointed to an item in the glass casing.

Savannah seemed even more uneasy. He noticed the tension in her shoulders and the pinched look on her face. He also observed her relief when Bobby turned to walk away. She exhaled slowly and rolled her shoulders like she was trying to break up the tension.

With a to-go box in his hand, Bobby kept his gaze on the floor and slinked out of the bakery.

After Savannah had helped everyone else in line, Liam hoped she'd return to his table. She didn't. Since she wasn't likely to pluck up the courage to approach him twice, he figured it was his turn to make a move.

"Need a refill?" She pre-empted as he approached the counter.

Since his coffee mug wasn't in his hand, he couldn't help but chuckle. "I wondered if you'd like to take a walk after your shift later."

A split-second of hesitation told him he wasn't too off base in asking her out. She followed up with a hard, "Thanks, but that's not a good idea."

Savannah's heart felt like it might pound its way out of her chest with Liam standing across the counter. For a split-second when he'd asked her out, she desperately wanted to say yes.

"Too bad. I had some time to kill before my meeting and I figured you could use a friend being new to town."

Liam's disappointment shouldn't impact Savannah one way or the other. Technically, she didn't know him from Adam. So, what was happening with the guilty feeling settling in her chest?

"I'm sorry. I just—"

His hand came up to stop her.

"No need to make up an excuse. I'm a big boy." There was an edge of hurt to his voice that he seemed like he was trying to cover. He recovered quickly when he said, "I can walk alone just as easy."

The word *alone* resonated with Savannah. It was pretty much how she'd spent all her time for the past year and it had been the loneliest twelve months of her life since her parent's deaths. She'd been able to rebuild her life in Austin because many of her friends also attended the same college as her, but after four years they'd all moved to other cities for work. Leo, her engineering friend, got an offer at a popular internet search engine company in California. He'd soon fallen out of touch after embracing the live-at-work lifestyle that came with the job. Her friend, April, had moved to Atlanta for work and to be near her boyfriend. The two were now married with a kid.

Jenny...*Jenny*.

Savannah couldn't think about her friend in any capacity without tears threatening. She couldn't even allow herself to think about Jenny's family. How they must feel after losing their daughter. She could only imagine the heartache they experienced on a daily basis. No parent should ever lose a child. It went against the natural order of life. And, although Savannah had only met the Dixons on the day Jenny had moved in to the apartment and then at Jenny's funeral, they seemed like nice people who definitely didn't deserve to lose their only daughter.

Savannah had reached out twice since the funeral. Neither attempt to connect had been fruitful. She couldn't blame them. All she could think was that she most likely reminded them of what had to have been the worst day of their lives. She'd decided to give it some time before trying again. Weeks had stretched into months. And now it just seemed out of place to try.

And then there was the fact that Savannah had been living in Gunner for a few weeks now and had only seen the bakery, the inside of her aunt's house, and the grocery store.

Aunt Becky knew Liam and he seemed like a genuinely good person. A piece of her wanted to get to know him better.

Once again, she locked gazes with Liam and with a confidence she didn't yet feel asked, "What time do you want to meet?"

"What time does the bakery close?" If he was shocked, he didn't show it.

"I can be out of here by two-thirty."

"How does three o'clock sound?" His voice was as casual as anybody pleased. He had the kind of deep timbre that sent warmth to places long neglected.

She stared at him for a long moment, debating whether or not a walk with Liam Quinn was more than she could handle. "Three-thirty?"

"It's a date." He flashed a smile at her that under normal circumstances would've turned her insides to quivering mush before saying, "Correction, it's a meeting."

"Where would you like to *meet*?" She put extra emphasis on the last word as she returned the smile.

He sat there looking like he needed a minute to think about the answer to that question. There was something in his eyes that said she wasn't the only one with a past. Pain? Hurt? Maybe that was half the appeal of a man like Liam Quinn. Kindred spirits?

Savannah almost laughed out loud. The man was sinning-on-Sunday gorgeous and all she could think about was the sadness in his eyes. Granted, it had been a long time since she'd gone out with anyone she found interesting. But she was seriously rusty if that was her focus when she was in the same room with a hot guy like Liam.

It might be nice to get to know someone different for a change. She was pretty certain she'd never spent time with a millionaire cattle rancher's son, especially one who'd chucked the family business to move out of town and work on someone else's cattle ranch. She was intrigued, figuring there had to be a story there. And, besides, she could use all the new friends she could get in her life right now.

And there was no threat that she'd develop real feelings for him, because he didn't plan to stick around long enough.

She picked up her rag and moved away from the nearby tables back to his. Liam followed, taking a seat across from her.

"There's a park not too far from here, Klyde Park. Not too many people go there, or at least they didn't use to." He stopped when he got a good look at her face. She didn't like being so transparent. But the thought of being alone with anyone in a park caused her to tremble.

"Or we could go somewhere else. Anywhere else. I have a large family that, to be perfectly honest, I wouldn't mind avoiding today."

She cocked an eyebrow at him and tilted her head. "I thought you came here to see your family."

"It's complicated. My family is complicated. And I just don't feel like doing complicated today."

"Won't they know you're in town and trying to avoid them?"

He cracked a smile. "They won't know if you don't tell them."

Savannah couldn't help but laugh. She put her arms in the air, palms up in the surrender position. "They won't hear the news from me."

This close, she could see the brilliant pale blue color of his eyes. The stubble on his face made her want to smooth her hand across it and feel the roughness. But those eyes were the show-stealer. They were like looking into the most crystal-clear water. There was an honesty in them she had never seen before in another person's. Their depths made her feel like she could gaze into them forever and never completely understand the man who owned them.

Suddenly, he reached for his empty coffee mug. She flinched before she caught herself. She hoped he would let her slip up get right past him. His hand froze. Those blue eyes seemed to take in everything.

"I'm just picking up my empty cup. Didn't mean to cause you any alarm."

"You didn't." The look he shot her said he wasn't buying the lie. She wasn't lying to him on purpose, so much as just thinking out loud. Granted, it was wishful thinking. But from deep in her soul she wanted it to be true. "You did." She hesitated before looking him square in the eye. "I'm a work in progress on that."

"I've got no problem moving slow." And he did just that when he stood. She was reminded just how tall and strong he was when she saw the thin cotton of his shirt stretch over a broad chest as he moved. Somehow, sitting down, he didn't look quite this big.

She didn't notice now out of fear. It was quite the opposite. She figured being alone anywhere with him she'd still be safe and she hadn't felt that way in more than a year. A piece of her wanted to grab hold of it, hang on to it, and never let go.

Since that was about as realistic as an accountant taking a vacation during tax season, she stood up, smiled at him and took a step back from the table.

Liam's eyebrows shot up.

"Will I see you at three-thirty?"

"I'll be there."

4

L iam found himself with a quite a few hours to kill and no
desire to go to the ranch. He did, however, want to see his
twin, Isaac. He walked outside and fished his cell out of his
pocket. After scrolling through his contacts, he tapped on his brother's name.

"I heard you were in town," Isaac answered before the second
ring.

"How in the world did you know I was in Gunner?" Liam
should've known. He'd received more than his fair share of second
looks in line this morning. News in a small town was like gasoline to a
forest fire, it spread quickly.

"Ran into Dan Brant at the feed store earlier. He performed a
double take, and then he came over and asked me how I beat him
here when I was behind him in line at the bakery. There was pretty
much only one explanation after that."

Good point. "You got me there."

"When did you get in?" Isaac didn't ask where Liam had been or
why he hadn't returned calls. Isaac, of all people, knew Liam. Something he was beyond grateful for.

In Colorado, there was something nice about not being recognized as a Quinn and God knew he was more than okay with leaving behind his bad memories at the ranch. But after growing up in a town where everyone knew each other on a first name basis, he'd had a difficult time getting used to anonymity.

"Last night or technically this morning depending on your viewpoint."

"Welcome home, brother."

"I'm just passing through." Liam wanted to make the point clear.

"Even so." Isaac quieted and Liam figured his brother waited for him to make a move. Isaac had always had patience that seemed to have skipped over Liam. No one would ever say that Liam was a patient man.

And since he didn't want to make this phone call all about him, he decided to change course. Besides, his brother had had a major life change.

"Congratulations, Isaac. Gina must be one helluva person for you to get married in a matter of days and entertain sticking around Gunner." All three of them had grown up together and gone to the same high school. Liam hadn't spent much time around Gina back then even though she'd dated his brother. From what he knew of her, she was kind, pretty, and exactly his brother's type. The two had dated for a short time before Isaac became moody, shut himself off from the world, and then signed up for the military the day he turned eighteen.

"Thank you. She is." Isaac paused.

"I'm happy for you, man. I really am." Liam's painful past had no bearing on how he felt toward his brother and his new wife. "You don't have to walk on eggshells."

"That means a lot, Liam." The relief was evident in his brother's tone.

"What's your take on T.J.?" Liam changed the subject. He didn't want to bring his brother's mood down, and he needed to set his own mind at ease before facing the rest of the family.

"Neither myself, Noah nor Eli can figure out what's wrong with him. Noah saw him with a fistful of pills in the kitchen the other morning. Couldn't tell if they were vitamins or medication and T.J. didn't volunteer information."

Eli and Noah had been the only ones to stay on at the ranch after the rest of them had moved away.

"What do *you* think?" His brother's opinion was important.

"I haven't been back long enough to get a good read on him. The only thing I can tell you for certain is that he's different now."

"Meaning what? He pops pills in the morning? Those could be vitamins. As strange as it is to admit the man is getting older; it's not an uncommon need."

"He skips the four-thirty a.m. barn meeting on a regular basis."

That information was alarming. Liam took a minute to let the news sink in. T.J. had always been about the ranch. He put business before everything else, including his own family. While his father always seemed to have a lady friend to go out with, the man had never remarried. In fact, they'd always joked T.J. was married to the ranch. "When did this start happening?"

"According to Eli, it's been going on for weeks. Noah almost fell over when he walked into the kitchen and saw T.J. dressed in his pajamas long after sunrise."

"Damn." Those things combined were troublesome.

"Damn is right."

Liam hadn't been all that concerned about T.J. until this conversation. Was it enough to get past what had happened between them? The question was worth asking. Because a piece of Liam wanted to have a real relationship with his father.

Buck up and move on. His father's so-called words of encouragement echoed in Liam's thoughts. At twenty-five years old, he'd lost a wife and an unborn child and his father's response had been to tell him to buck up.

Come to think of it, the man had said those same words after Liam's mother had died. Cold-hearted was the tip of the iceberg when it came to describing T.J.'s attempts to comfort his mourning children. Liam's younger brothers had been too young to know what was happening. Not the elder Quinns. All they'd had for comfort was each other.

Liam didn't have it in him to *buck up* then and he didn't need to be reminded now. Those words had driven a wedge between him and his father at age seven. The wedge had turned into a cavern by age twenty-five. And now it just seemed like too far to build a bridge.

In theory, it should have made hearing the news that T.J. might be terminally sick a bit like finding out an uncle he'd never known died. It was a surprising blow that it felt like Liam had been gut-punched by the theory. He reminded himself that it was just that...a theory. And did what he did best, tucked his feelings of distress down deep and prayed they didn't surface again.

"Will I see you at the ranch later?"

Liam had anticipated the question. He should have an answer for Isaac. He didn't. "Do you have any idea when the others are coming to town?"

"Good question. I didn't even know you were here until Dan." The jab was fair.

"This is as close as I can come right now."

Isaac's voice lowered, and his tone had all the compassion in the world when he said, "I understand. We can wait until the others arrive if you want. Set up the meeting in town. There's no reason to have it at Quinnland. The important thing is to hear the news together. I think that's what means the most to T.J."

"If he's sick, do you think he's trying to manipulate us with his will? Tell us who is getting what? Because I don't want anything from him." Liam hadn't thought about it until now, but it would be just like the old T.J. to drag everyone together just to let them know how much they'd disappointed him. Only two of his sons had stayed on at the ranch. And until this phone call, Liam had been pretty certain that Noah wouldn't be caught dead in the same room with their father.

"I could be off base. But Noah and Eli are on the same track as I am. T.J. is acting different toward us. What that means is anybody's guess, but he seems genuinely concerned about connecting with us. He's making an effort with my wife and daughter that appears to come from the heart. I'm willing to ride it out and see where this goes."

When he heard the words *wife* and *daughter,* Liam felt like a jerk. He'd been so annoyed with T.J. that he hadn't asked his brother about the new baby girl he was adopting.

"On that note, I'm happy for you, man. A daughter must be an amazing thing to have." A stab of pain knifed Liam in thinking about what had been taken from him. He pushed through it because Isaac deserved to be happy.

"Everly is a sweet kid." There was so much pride in Isaac's voice that it caught Liam off guard. He and his twin used to be so close they used to joke they could practically hear each other's thoughts. It didn't seem right that Isaac's life had changed so much and Liam hadn't been around to witness it.

"Hey, I'm sorry about not coming to the wedding."

"We should've taken it off-site."

"It's not your fault I've been an asshole. My mail has been piling up and I rarely check my phone. By the time I realized what was going on, I'd missed it." Isaac had texted the developments in his life. Liam needed to step up and do right by his brother.

"For what it's worth, I never doubted that you care. We have a bond no one can break and especially not T.J." They both knew how often their father had tried to pit his sons against each other when they were young. It had only made them closer. "Don't force yourself to do anything out of some false sense of loyalty to me. I know where we stand. When and if you're ready to come back to Quinn-land, I'll be here. If the day never comes, I'll meet you anywhere you want. When and if you're ready to meet my family, they'll be around."

"I'm staying at the Gunner Inn next door to the bakery." Liam struggled with getting out his next words and not because he wasn't ecstatic for Isaac. "I'd like to meet your family, Isaac."

"Name the time. We'll be there." There was a hint of bridled enthusiasm in Isaac's voice and it struck Liam how selfish he'd been.

Granted, it was a strange turn of events that had Isaac becoming a father before Liam. Still, he was nothing but happy for his brother. From the sounds of it, Isaac had found true love and that was rare.

"Can I get back to you on filling in the details?" Thinking about a family always brought him back to Lynn. His wife had been five months pregnant when the tractor accident happened that had taken her life, the life of Liam's unborn child had left him with a hole in his chest, along with a scar from his collarbone to underarm.

Waking up in the hospital, learning he'd been the only survivor that day, had made him want to die. He couldn't think about another child without remembering his son. It dawned on him that it might be that loss, and not the thought of seeing T.J. again, that might be the reason it had been hard to imagine facing Quinnland again.

"Of course." Isaac seemed to work hard to hide the disappointment in his voice. If Liam didn't know his brother as well as he knew himself, he might've missed it.

"I'm proud of you, Isaac."

"That means a lot, Liam."

Because of their bond, Liam would dig deep and find the courage to meet his brother's family. He had to find a way.

SAVANNAH STEPPED a little lighter for the rest of her shift. In an unexpected twist, she actually found herself thinking about Liam Quinn and looking forward to seeing him got her through the lunch rush.

Life could change on a dime, she thought, as she peeked her head into her aunt's office where she was tallying up the day's deposit.

"I'm taking off now." She always liked to let Aunt Becky know before she left.

Aunt Becky blinked up at her in shock. "You don't want to wait for me to finish getting the deposit ready?"

"I'm good."

Aunt Becky's gaze widened. "You sure about that? I won't be long."

"I am. I've been thinking it's silly for me to follow behind you in my own car everywhere we go. You go make the deposit on your own.

You don't need a shadow." She glanced at the stack of envelopes that needed to go to the post office. "I can drop those off on my way home."

Aunt Becky's mouth nearly dropped to her desk. She recovered. "You're positive?"

Savannah nodded and couldn't help but laugh a little bit. "I probably won't be home until later."

The reason seemed to dawn on Aunt Becky when she rocked her head and winked. "Does Liam Quinn have anything to do with why you'll be late?"

"Maybe." Savannah smiled a real smile. Not like the ones she'd learned to plaster on her face so people who cared about her would stop looking at her like she might flip out at any minute.

Aunt Becky picked up the stack of mail and thrust it toward her. Her ear-to-ear grin said she approved. "Have fun with that."

"We're meeting at Klyde Park."

She rocked her head. "I know the one you're talking about. Beautiful park. Not too busy. There are usually a couple of joggers. No playground, so no little tykes running around." She shoved Savannah toward the door. "Go on. You don't want to be late."

"Aunt Becky, if I didn't know you better, I'd say you were trying to get rid of me." God, it felt good to laugh again. It felt good to look forward to something again. It felt good to shed her fears and rejoin the world even if it was just baby steps.

"I am. Now, scoot." Aunt Becky's blue eyes were so much like Savannah's mother's. They twinkled with mischief now and Savannah was happy for a break from all the tension.

"Should I wear the floral skirt or jeans?"

"It's April, so you can't go wrong with flowers." She put her finger to her lips. "On second thought, what's the temperature out there?"

"It was supposed to warm up but I'm not sure it ever did."

"Then jeans. You can borrow my boots. The ones with the teal inlay." She popped her shoulder toward her chin and wiggled her eyebrows.

"Those are your favorites. I can't take those."

"This is a special occasion. And a special occasion calls for special boots." Aunt Becky stood and took Savannah's hand in hers. She led her around the office in a waltz. "Mr. Stillwater and I had quite a few dates in the park you're going to."

Savannah was sorry she hadn't been closer to her aunt while growing up. The two had connected after Savannah's parents died. Since then, she'd heard so many wonderful stories about her uncle. It was a shame she'd never met him.

"I love when you talk about him." She and her aunt had stayed up way past bedtime on the occasions Savannah had come to visit during college. She'd sleep the next day while her aunt somehow managed to wake up at the crack of dawn to open the bakery.

"You go make some of your own. And do something worth retelling over popcorn."

Savannah laughed. Popcorn always came with juicy stories about Aunt Becky's past, and what a past it had been.

"I'll see what I can do." She grabbed her purse from the drawer and walked out the front, locking the door behind her.

As she turned, she caught the glint of copper at her feet. She bent down to pick up the lucky penny, holding it her palm for a long moment, hoping it was her lucky day. And then she dropped it into the bottom of her purse so she'd have it with her.

Bobby Raider rounded the corner.

For some reason, Savannah gasped. She told herself he'd caught her off guard and that was a little bit true. Mostly, the guy just creeped her out. He'd been stopping by the bakery every morning since her second day. He never really talked to her, yet he seemed to be watching her every time she looked over at him. He wasn't a large man and there wasn't anything blatantly scary about him. She tried to convince herself he wasn't that bad as she tucked her chin to her chest and walked past him.

She clicked the key fob and slid into the driver's seat, making sure Bobby hadn't followed her. Checking over her shoulder had become a ritual after Harley Patterson, but she didn't want to think about the past tonight.

After cranking the engine, she drove straight to the post office. Normally, she ran the errand with Aunt Becky, who'd introduced her around. Being on her own scared and excited her. The hint of possibility caused a ripple of anticipation. The sun was out even though it was chilly. There were white puffy clouds dotting the sky, forming shapes she'd spent a great deal of her childhood examining. Naming.

With the window cracked, she got just enough cool air on her face to breathe new life into her.

After depositing the outgoing mail in the box, she winded down the country road leading to Aunt Becky's house on the outskirts of town. When Mr. Stillwater had been alive, he and her aunt had owned horses. Aunt Becky said she spent too many hours at the bakery to handle them on her own, so as his horses crossed over the rainbow bridge she didn't replace them.

The small barn behind the two-story farmhouse was always kept clean and ready though. Aunt Becky had said it was her tribute to her late husband and the least she could do. She claimed to be too old to care for the place herself, so she paid a neighbor's high school-aged son to come twice a week to keep the spiders at bay.

The neighbor, Craig Whittaker, was six-feet of football player brawn. He dropped by on Mondays and Thursdays after school now that football season was technically over. And again on Sunday nights but Aunt Becky only paid him for two days. She said she believed he'd added the extra night to have a place to get away from home since his stepfather had moved back in. Craig was a smart kid with an unhappy home life, according to her aunt.

To Savannah's thinking, he was stand-offish and came across as a little arrogant. Her aunt had blamed his age, hormones. Savannah hadn't spent enough time around teenagers to know any different. And hearing about his home life softened her attitude toward him. She'd had wonderful parents and missed them to this day.

She did, however, have some experience with high school football players, having grown up under Friday night lights. She knew full well the demands a coach could make on players. And how arrogant a good player could be. She'd dated the star running back for a short time before the head cheerleader set her sights on him. Brainy Savannah didn't have a fighting chance against well-developed Hannah Razor.

It had all turned out fine. Her relationship with the high school running back wouldn't have gone anywhere, Savannah mused. Dating someone so different from her had been a novelty. After a few dates, the shine had already started wearing off anyway. So, technically, Hannah had done her a favor.

As for Craig, Savannah would take a wait-and-see approach. A voice in the back of her head told her she wouldn't trust any man after what had happened. Maybe that was true. Or maybe her instincts about Craig were right. Either way, she did her best to avoid him when he showed up at the back door to get paid every week.

As she neared the turn-off for her aunt's street, a deer darted onto the farm road from out of the tree line. Savannah veered, making a hard right. She missed the deer and ended up in the ditch. Gearshift in reverse, she tamped down the panic rising in her chest. Foot on gas pedal, she tried to back out of the ditch. Her tires spun, kicking up mud everywhere but gaining zero traction.

From behind her, she heard the whir of a vintage truck's engine coming closer on the narrow road. Savannah craned her neck, turning her torso to get a better look.

There was a single person in the vehicle. Male. Large. From this distance, she couldn't identify the driver.

Rational thought flew out the window as she reached for the door handle. With her right hand, she cut off the engine, dropped her keys in her purse and then grabbed the straps of her handbag. Throwing her shoulder into the driver's side, she pulled the lever. Her breathing came in gasps and all she could think about was getting the hell away from there.

5

Savannah didn't turn around. Not when the black truck's brakes groaned to a stop. Not even when the driver shouted. In fact, the strong male voice made her run even harder. Instincts had kicked in, pure fight or flight mode, and there was no stopping her.

"Wait. Hold on there."

She didn't recognize the male voice, so she pushed her legs harder. Properties in this area came with lots that could span multiple acres. Aunt Becky's farmhouse was at least a few miles away. There was no way Savannah could get there on foot and especially since she didn't have her bearings in this area. Too afraid to turn around and head back, she bolted toward the thicket.

A thought struck. Had she turned her car off?

Panic was a strange thing. Her flight instinct had kicked in and she couldn't honestly remember. Her heart pounded, thinking about being alone on a country road with a strange man. Images of the night a year ago assaulted her and her chest squeezed so tightly it felt like her heart might burst. She risked another glance behind her to see if the large male had followed her.

Thankfully, she couldn't see any trace of him and she prayed that was a good sign. Common sense dictated that even *if* he'd been following her in the first place, the chain of events that led her to abandon her car had a low probability. The odds were in her favor the man was genuinely trying to help.

Tell that to her irrational fears.

She'd reached the thicket, so she darted in and around trees in the hopes they'd cover her. If the stranger had somehow followed her, she had a chance at losing him. Her foot caught in the underbrush, she tripped and almost face planted. A tree branch slapped her shoulder as she took a couple of steps to right herself. She clawed for purchase on a tree trunk. In the process, she let go of her purse strap. It went flying. Contents spilled out.

Down on all fours, trying to scoop her belongings into her bag, her hand raked over her keys. Thank God for small miracles. She grabbed those and everything else she could find as she surveyed the area.

There was no sign of the large male driver of the truck. She pushed up to her feet and ran a little farther, ducking around branches and swerving to miss trees.

The only bright spot in any of this scenario was that she'd had the presence of mind to turn her car engine off. Savannah's thighs burned. The sound of a twig snapping to her left caught her attention. She glanced around, checking to see if the large male was there. He wasn't. The noise could've come from an animal.

An icy chill ran down her spine. She couldn't decide what was worse, being stalked by a man or trapped by an animal.

When she was certain she was alone—and only then—she slowed her pace enough to dig inside her purse. Sweat covered her despite the chilly air and her breathing was so hard she was starting to get lightheaded. Savannah wondered how runners pushed through this feeling because all it made her want to do was stop. Her fingers closed around her cell phone. She said a little prayer there'd be service.

After checking the screen, she saw that there were no bars.

It was probably too much to hope she'd have cell service out here. Besides, who would she call and what would she say?

Heart pounding her ribs in painful stabs, Savannah stopped. She squatted down and tried to catch her breath. She hugged her knees wondering if there'd ever be a day when she didn't panic over what sometimes felt like the slightest things.

Anger burned inside, not just for what Harley Patterson had done to Jenny but what he'd taken from Savannah in the process. He'd taken her friend and he'd taken away her ability to function like a normal person.

No longer could she live alone and feel safe. No longer could she take a walk outside on a nice day without constantly looking over her shoulder or listening for the sound of footsteps too close behind her. No longer could she look at people, and especially men, without constantly evaluating threat or looking for a quick escape.

Every building she walked into now, she had to memorize the exits. Before she moved into a neighborhood, she checked crime reports. Even that didn't stop her heart from racing every time she walked by an unfamiliar man in the streets.

She sized everyone up. The habit she'd developed last year stayed with her. It was one she was certain would be present for a long time to come. Possibly forever.

There'd been one person who didn't make her throat feel like it was closing when she tried to talk to him. Liam Quinn. Surprisingly, she hadn't flinched when he'd sat across from her. It was a shock when she really thought about it.

Rocking back and forth, she surveyed the area again. The wind blew right through her shirt and to her core. The temperatures had dropped, she had no idea when. Sounds she couldn't easily identify made the hair on the back of her neck prick. Out here, she was even more alone.

Figuring she was worse off in the thicket than she'd been in her car, she pushed to standing. Her legs were a little wobbly from exertion. At her vehicle, she could roll up the windows and lock the doors. Maybe even get a bar or two and make a call for help. She would've appreciated having those thoughts twenty minutes ago instead of acting on pure impulse.

Aunt Becky would be coming home soon, and she'd pass right by Savannah's car. Her aunt would be worried if she saw it in a ditch on the side of the road, and especially without hearing from her to know that she was okay.

The overwhelming feeling she'd grossly overreacted engulfed her. Embarrassment followed because the reality struck that she'd abandoned her vehicle without a word and some poor local probably stood there bewildered, wondering what on earth she was thinking.

Savannah took in a deep breath and started to backtrack toward her vehicle. She took note that this area consisted mostly of fields, trees and the occasional house. When she got her own place, she'd like to be closer to town. She'd told her aunt to move now that she lived alone but Aunt Becky could dig her heels in when she felt strongly about something. Leaving the house meant saying a final goodbye to the place where she'd lived with her husband. Even though he'd passed away several years ago and the house was too much to take care of on her own, Aunt Becky couldn't take that step.

The air had cooled in the last twenty minutes or maybe Savannah's body cooled after being drenched with sweat. Either way, she shivered as she made the trek back to her car. She didn't realize she'd gone so far. As she moved through the trees, sound amplified. Leaves rustling seemed twice as noisy and sent her pulse racing. She thought about all the wild animals that could be stalking her.

When she finally broke the tree line there was a bevy of vehicles around hers. Aunt Becky was there, just as Savannah had feared.

"I'm here." She waved her arms wildly. Her legs wouldn't support another run.

Aunt Becky put her hand over her heart as she started toward Savannah. The sheer look of panic on her aunt's face sent a wave of guilt washing over her.

"What happened?"

"I'm sorry. I didn't have a way to reach you. I swerved to miss a deer and ended up in the ditch. Someone stopped, a man, and I panicked." Hearing the words brought home the fact she didn't want to be scared anymore. It was time to take her life back. More baby steps.

Before she could say anything else, she was being pulled into an embrace. "You're okay."

Savannah had never wanted to believe two words more in her life. She held onto her aunt as the tow truck driver hauled her vehicle onto the road and set it straight again.

Once it was ready to go, Aunt Becky released her. "There was no one here when I drove by. Who did you say stopped?"

Savannah shrugged. "I didn't get a good look at the driver. All I know is he was a large man. I didn't stick around long enough to get a better description."

"You're as pale as a ghost," Aunt Becky said. "Do you want to follow me home?"

It occurred to Savannah that she would be late to the park now, late to see Liam and she'd forgotten to get his number.

"I should go into town." There was no time to change or get the bakery smell off her clothes. The fact she'd had no time to change or put on makeup didn't matter.

She wanted to see Liam.

～

"YOU'RE STILL HERE. I'm so late."

Liam pushed to standing from the park bench he'd been sitting on. One look at Savannah's wild eyes and apologetic features said she'd been through hell. Her shoes were caked with mud and it looked like she'd just run a marathon. She had on the same clothes as she'd worn at the bakery, not that he minded. She would be beautiful wearing a potato sack.

"What happened?" To be honest, he wasn't sure she would show and didn't take it personally after seeing how many times she'd jumped over little noises at the bakery earlier that morning. She had demons. He had ghosts.

"May I sit?" Her voice had the effect of listening to a slow jazz rhythm.

"Sure. It's only been fifteen minutes." He shrugged a shoulder and studied her as she took a seat on the opposite end of the bench from him. He sat down on his side, not encroaching on her comfort zone.

"I'm still sorry. I was worried you'd think I didn't want to be here." In fact, he figured she was being pretty damn brave stretching out of her comfort zone to agree to seeing him at all. "I ended up in a ditch to avoid hitting a deer, and needed a tow."

The cool breeze on his face and the reminders of happier times at this very park with his brothers had improved his mood. Her showing up was a bonus as far as he was concerned. The dark clouds had returned after dredging up memories during his conversation with his brother and Liam had needed to be reminded of good times in Gunner.

Savannah wasn't the only one with baggage.

"Do you want to talk about it?" He knew full-well she'd avoided his question about what had happened. He took it as a sign she wasn't ready to talk about it.

"I have a past." A breeze blew, wafting the smell of coffee and fresh baked bread. He'd never thought of bread as especially sexy until that moment.

Instead of asking questions, he waited for her to explain figuring she'd tell him what she was comfortable sharing.

"Talking about it won't make it go away. I've tried. Best counselor in Austin couldn't stop me from jumping at every noise." She put her hand on his arm and he ignored the frisson of heat along with the unexpected stirring of attraction that came with contact. "I'm here. This is a big step for me. I totally understand if dealing with this is too much for you. We hardly know each other and have no history that would tell you I'm actually not a crazy person."

"Didn't think you were."

Savannah withdrew her hand almost like she'd touched fire. "Would it be okay if we changed the subject?"

"How about them Cowboys?"

She laughed and he was glad to put a smile on her face.

Then, she turned the tables. "Did you grow up in Gunner?"

"Yes."

"Seems like a nice place. The people have been really welcoming."

He agreed with her assessment, so he nodded. He also didn't see the need to point out that Gunner had plenty of single men, many of whom had been in line at the bakery this morning. The fact that she was a beautiful and single woman could bring out extra charm from Gunner's male residents.

"Mind if I ask why you left?"

Liam shrugged. "Didn't want to work for the family business and I'm a damn fine cattle rancher."

"Oh, really? Why do you work in another state?" The tension radiating from her eased a few notches when she exhaled.

The question made him smile.

"It's complicated."

6

"It's complicated? Is that code for not wanting to talk about it?"

Well, now Liam really chuckled.

"You got me there."

She scooted toward him, moving close enough to bump his shoulder with hers. More of that unexpected attraction stirred and he had to quash it.

"That's a good line, though. Mind if I borrow it?" She beamed at him.

"Be my guest. It's fair game." Liam laughed outright and unapologetic. He was grateful her stress seemed to ease, and he hoped being with him had something to do with it. He glanced over at her as she looked out at the rolling hills and sighed. The breeze toyed with her golden hair that was still tied back in a ponytail. She took in a deep breath and then exhaled. "This park is beautiful. It's so close to town and I've never even heard of it before today."

"One of my favorites." He pointed toward a smattering of trees. "Me and my brothers used to play hide-and-seek over there when we weren't much bigger than those bushes."

"How many brothers do you have?"

"Six brothers and five cousins. All boys."

"Twelve boys?" Savannah smacked her knee. "Wow. I can't imagine how your parents kept up with seven children let alone add five cousins to the mix."

Liam waited for it. He waited for the joke that was sure to come.

"You know that's enough guys to fill an entire calendar."

Liam chuckled again, the low rumble came from deep in his chest.

"You've heard that before, haven't you?" She was smart and perceptive. Those were traits he admired.

Liam nodded. "More than a few times."

"Sorry." She flashed those beautiful amber eyes at him and his heart squeezed. He'd dated his share of women in the years since the accident but had always figured that something had broken with his wife's death, because not one person had caused a reaction anywhere near this scale. It was almost a shame he had no plans to stick around Gunner.

"Don't be. It never sounded as funny when other people said it." The fact the two of them were making easy conversation seemed like progress for Savannah. Liam wasn't sure why that soothed his soul other than it felt good to help someone when he'd been so damn bad at helping himself. There was something about Savannah that brought out his protective instincts and he liked making her feel at ease.

"Tell me about your family. Were you all close? Did everyone grow up in Gunner?" Her eyes brightened making them even more brilliant and easier to look into.

"Very close. All of us. Now, we're spread across Texas and Colorado. What about you? Do you have any siblings?" He managed to turn the tables.

"No. It was just me and my parents. We lived in Austin where my mother taught pre-school and my father worked as a law clerk."

"No cousins?"

She shrugged and responded with a vulnerable smile. Their eyes connected, sending a jolt of awareness rocketing through him. Looking at Savannah was very easy on the eyes, but he needed to get a handle on his physical reaction to her. Liam didn't do sex for sex's sake, and even if he did she couldn't even sit next to him for longer than two seconds, let alone have full-on physical contact.

"Aunt Becky is my mom's only living relative. She used to visit us on holidays before she married. She and her husband never had children of their own and she used to joke that I was all she had to take care of her in her old age."

"I can't imagine your aunt ever slowing down; she has more energy than people half her age. The bakery has been around ever since I can remember. Our caregiver used to bring us into town on Sundays to visit the bakery and then come to the park." Liam relaxed against the seat and rested his right ankle on top of his left knee. "Your aunt always welcomed us with open arms."

"She's a saint. Aunt Becky pretty much saved my life when my parents died."

"I'm sorry to hear about your parents. It's not easy losing family so young." He knew firsthand. Based on the sound of her voice, she'd never gotten over the loss. He could relate to the feeling. Another arbitrary thought struck. Savannah had had ties to Gunner and by sheer coincidence had never spent time there.

"Thank you, Liam." There was so much sincerity in her voice.

"It's early, but do you want to grab something to eat?" Waking up so early in the morning meant he was ready for dinner by four o'clock.

"I could eat. It seems like bakers and ranchers keep similar hours." Another one of those smiles and his heart took another shot.

"You want to go in some place or do a drive-thru?"

"Given the fact you aren't ready to be seen in town—"

He shot her a surprised look.

"Yes, I noticed this morning at the bakery. You kept your head low and genuinely seemed disappointed that my aunt recognized you."

He laughed. "You got me. I just wanted fresh coffee and breakfast. Most folks figured I was my brother and I didn't make an effort to correct them. My brother has been home a short while and everyone has gotten used to seeing him again."

"Where'd he come home from?"

"The Middle East. He's been serving his country for the past fourteen years and I couldn't be prouder of him." He checked her ring finger, looking for a tan line or some indication she'd been married. She couldn't still be attached to someone, or she wouldn't be there with him. She seemed like the type of person who would take her vows seriously.

"I'll have to thank him for his service the next time I see him." The hint of pride in her voice caused Liam's chest to swell.

"He'd never ask for it, but I know he'd appreciate the kindness."

Her brow furrowed. "Was that hard for you? When he left?"

He rocked his head. "We'd been joined at the hip for eighteen years. It was a shock to the system to say the least, but it's the best thing that ever happened to us. We needed separate identities. Folks always lumped us together as one person before. I might not have believed it at the time but we needed the break."

Isaac had flown home the minute he'd heard about the accident. He'd had to return to the Middle East a few days later, but Liam practically forced Isaac to go sooner. They'd already been apart for seven years and Liam had gotten good at shutting people out. He'd somehow convinced Isaac to give him space, which turned into a divide between them. Hell, Liam had broken contact with all of his brothers and cousins after the accident.

"I can't imagine what it must be like to grow up with such a big family."

"Crazy." Liam couldn't emphasize the word enough. But also great. He'd never had to look far to have someone to hang out with and his brothers always had his back. "There was a lot of wrestling. We were competitive about just about everything. I couldn't have asked for better brothers, though."

Talking to Savannah made Liam realize how fortunate he was to have as much family as he did. His and T.J.'s relationship might be complicated, but the man was still alive. And if the thoughts circulating among family members had merit, T.J. might not be around for long.

The finality of that thought struck Liam hard.

Savannah glanced around, shifting on the bench. The air changed between them or maybe it was just tension had started radiating from her.

"What's wrong?"

"Nothing. Everything's okay." She scanned the lot behind them, sounding like she was trying to convince herself of the fact. Her hands twisted together on her lap.

"Do you get the sense someone's watching us?"

Liam might not feel a threat but based on Savannah's expression, she did. He surveyed the area and didn't see anything or anyone who sounded any alarm bells. Leaves rustled the trees. A couple walked arm-in-arm on the walking path. Those two were the closest to where he and Savannah sat.

Glancing behind him, he noticed about a half dozen cars in the lot. Liam saw dried mud on a bumper and figured that vehicle must belong to Savannah.

A few random folks dotted the path, walkers or joggers. This was a good place for off-road hiking. A man had a dog with him. Liam didn't notice anything out of the ordinary.

He didn't want Savannah to think he didn't believe her. "Nothing strikes me as odd so far, but I'll keep my eyes peeled just in case." He motioned toward the trail. "You want to get up and take a walk or head out to dinner?"

She was on her feet in a heartbeat. "A walk sounds good."

"I'll keep an eye out behind us if you want to keep your gaze to the front." He wanted to offer some reassurance. Call it Cowboy Code or protective instincts but he wanted to give her peace of mind.

He understood devastation, loss. He understood the feeling of having everything taken away from him in a snap. And it was probably the same look of devastation in her eyes that he connected with. The broken parts in her were so familiar.

She nodded, keeping a little closer to his side as they moved toward the path. He offered an arm out of courtesy and, to his surprise, she took it.

"Thank you for not looking at me like I've lost my mind." Her voice was so quiet that he almost missed her words.

"You seem sane to me. Besides, I'm certain your Aunt Becky would have given me a heads-up if otherwise. " He smiled and winked.

She returned the smile and it put more of that pride in his chest that he seemed able to calm her.

"You were telling me about your family."

Liam figured he could give up a little about himself to gain her trust. If she trusted him, she'd open up more and he could get a better handle on the threat she felt.

"There's a reason I'm having a difficult time facing my family. It has nothing to do with my brothers but everything to do with the ranch and my father."

"Did something happen?"

"You could say that." Liam hadn't talked about his wife and unborn child to anyone. Ever. It had been seven years. *A long time*, a voice in the back of his mind pointed out. Maybe it was time to speak up.

"We don't have to talk about it if you don't want to. I know better than most about needing to keep some things inside."

"That's the thing, Savannah. I've been holding this in for seven years and it doesn't get any easier. I can't speak to what's best for you or your situation but being around you makes me *want* to tell you what happened in my past. You're easy to talk to. And I'm thinking it's high time I said the words out loud."

She didn't speak, but just squeezed his arm and he felt warmth in her touch that blazed a trail straight to his heart.

"I'm having trouble going back to the ranch. It's hard to face it. I can blame T.J. all I want. To be honest, it's not his fault." Liam thought back to his father's words. *Buck up and move on.* It's what his father did after Liam's mother died. He'd hardened his heart toward everyone and everything. He'd also lost out on having real relationships with his sons, but Liam wasn't so sure the fact mattered to his father all that much.

"What happened?" Her voice was the equivalent of a calm, gentle breeze on a sweltering day. The voice of someone who understood how difficult it would be to open up.

"Mine and my brothers' relationships had been strained with our father and we couldn't wait to leave Quinnland. My twin signed up for the military the day he turned eighteen and, if I'm honest, I missed him once he shipped out."

"That must've been crushing after spending your lives side-by-side. I've heard a lot about the twin bond. Sounds like that was true of the two of you."

"You could say that." Liam chuckled, thinking how inseparable the two of them had been growing up.

"You must've felt abandoned in some ways." She would probably know more than most, having lost her parents at such a young age. Even though it hadn't been his mother's fault, he'd experienced the very real feeling of being abandoned after her death.

"It made me lean on my girlfriend all that much more." Liam recalled the feelings like they were yesterday. "She got into University of Texas and it seemed like a good idea for me to follow her since I had nothing left here. We'd been sweethearts all through high school and I proposed on graduation day. We stayed engaged while she studied, and I worked just about every job under the sun to put her through school."

He paused and checked their surroundings, looking for signs of anything or anyone out of the ordinary. Satisfied everything was okay, he continued, "She got her nursing degree and a job at a teaching hospital in Austin. The weekend before she started work we went down to the justice of the peace and made our relationship official."

"I can't imagine you living in Austin and being happy."

"It was better than Gunner and far enough away from my father that I didn't risk running into him when I left the apartment. But, yeah, living in a crowded city wasn't my favorite thing." He was amazed she could read him so easily. "How'd you know that about me? We've only known each other a few hours."

"Ranching is in your blood. The reason you left had everything to do with your relationship with your father. You didn't mention anything about being unhappy with ranch life." She was observant.

"I would've rather waited until I was a bit older to take on as much responsibility as I had while growing up, but the rest is true enough."

"Plus, you work on a ranch now in a different state." Her face twisted in the cutest way when she highlighted her point.

"Some people would call that irony."

"I don't get the impression you chose your life's work to get back at your dad. If anything, you would've done the opposite to spite him."

Liam laughed out loud, and it helped break some of the tension inside him. Releasing something that had been pent up inside him for so long. "You mean work in a corporate building and put on a suit every day? That might've killed me instead."

Savannah's laugh had a musical quality to it he could get used to. Her smile lines softened when she quietly said, "You wouldn't have left her."

"No." He took his time saying the next words. "Even though we hardly ever saw each other working opposite shifts. Then there was this one time she took a night off and asked if we could talk. I thought she was planning to divorce me and was trying to find a way to break the news without crushing me. The relationship going south wasn't all her fault. I wasn't happy and I'm pretty certain I was hard to live with."

"A good marriage is hard to get off the ground when you don't have time for each other."

He nodded. He'd been naïve to think their history alone would keep her loyal to him while he figured his life out. Granted, the vows should've been some indication she was in it for the long haul. Best he could figure she got spooked when she realized he couldn't give her the life she wanted.

"Did she?" Savannah clarified the comment, "Divorce you?"

He shook his head. "She told me she was pregnant."

"Oh. That must've been a shock."

"You can say that again." Liam glanced at Savannah. "The bigger problem with her turning up pregnant was that we hadn't had sex in months."

7

"**A**re you saying what I think you are? The baby wasn't yours?"

He nodded.

Savannah covered her gasp with both hands. "I can only imagine what it must've been like for you. I'm so sorry."

"Don't be." Even though he offered reassurance, his heart told a different story. There was a well of sadness hidden there and yet unexplored pain that had been tucked away too long. Time had dulled some of what had been pure agony.

"Looking back, it wasn't all her fault. There was more I could've done, *should've* done to make our relationship work. I'd become selfish and stopped talking. She didn't know where to turn. We were both too young and too stupid to talk out our problems." Distance—and maybe maturity—had helped him put the situation in perspective.

"If she didn't divorce you, does that mean you're still married?" Confusion knitted her brows together as her gaze dropped to his ring finger.

"Not exactly. The father of her child had a wife of his own. He was a doctor at the hospital where she worked. He told her the affair was over and that he didn't want anything else to do with her or the baby. He told her he'd arrange for her to transfer out of his department and preferably to another hospital and that he'd provide financial support if she insisted on having the kid."

"How'd you take the news, Liam?"

"Hard, at first. I was hurt. I waited in the parking lot for the doctor at his sports car early one morning. Told him we didn't need his money and that he was off the hook. But if he hurt Lynn again or forced her out of a job she loved, that I'd be back for him."

"That was noble of you."

"Like I said, Lynn and I had known each other a long time. I couldn't leave her while she was depressed and pregnant. There was no way in hell I planned to tell anyone the child wasn't mine. I told her we'd figure out a way to work our relationship out. I could accept her son as mine. In retrospect, we might not have been 'in love' with each other but I loved her."

"I'm certain she felt the same about you."

He nodded, feeling some of the heavy weight he'd been carrying around for longer than he cared to remember start to break apart.

"We decided to stay together during the pregnancy and I planned to raise her child as my own. I think deep down we both knew it wouldn't work forever, but we were dedicated to putting the child's needs first. We figured we'd know when the timing was right to split. Hell, we were naïve enough to think we could fall in love with each other as a family unit and maybe things would work out after all."

"But that's not what happened?"

"Lynn got it in her head that after I was able to forgive her for her mistakes that me and T.J. should be able to reconcile our differences. She had this image of all of us as one happy family. She believed that if her and I could make something good out of the circumstances she'd messed up so badly, that her reconnecting me with my family would somehow be the silver lining."

"It's a nice thought but I'm not sure that's how it works."

"Exactly my thoughts when she pitched the idea." Liam would do things differently now if he could go back. He'd been too young, too naïve to understand all the implications in the way he did now. Loss had a way of maturing someone faster than nature intended. "We started making regular trips to the ranch to see my younger brothers and Marianne, our housekeeper."

"What about her family? You said the two of you met in high school, so they had to be local, right?" There was no hint of judgment in Savannah's voice, only compassion and understanding.

"She didn't get along with her parents and I think that was part of the reason she'd been so hell-bent on me reconnecting with T.J."

"It's always sad to hear people have parents who are alive but aren't close. Such a shame that her parents didn't appreciate their relationship with her any more than they did because if you loved her, she had to have been a good person at heart." He understood why family would be important to someone who'd lost hers at such a young age.

Liam took in a sharp breath. "She was five months along when she got on the back of the tractor. I'd told her to wait for me inside, but Lynn had a tendency to act first and ask questions later. Some might classify her behavior as reckless, and I wouldn't disagree on many counts, but once she came to terms with the pregnancy, she glowed. All she could talk about was our son. There's no way she would've put his life in danger if she'd realized what she was doing. But..."

His words cut off as Savannah covered another gasp with her hand. "I'm so sorry, Liam."

He didn't have to go into the gritty details of the accident or what he'd done to try to save his wife. "I wasn't thinking when I jumped in to try to save them. I was in the hospital for days before I regained consciousness. Then, of course, I learned that neither Lynn nor the baby survived. I don't remember much after that except feeling numb."

"No one should have to deal with that kind of loss. That's too much for someone so young to handle." She said other words meant to comfort and they were balm to a wounded soul.

Liam fisted his hands before forcing them to relax. "T.J.'s response when I was released from the hospital was to tell me to '*Buck up and move on.*'"

A tear tumbled down her cheek. "How could you after everything you'd lost?"

"I couldn't. He made me feel less-than for not being able to put their deaths behind me. I figured we wouldn't see eye-to-eye anytime soon, so I packed up and moved out of state to put more distance between me and him."

Realization seemed to dawn on her. "You haven't set foot on ranch property since, have you?"

He shook his head. Dredging up those painful memories should gut him. He hadn't been able to let them bubble up to the surface, let alone voice them, but talking to Savannah came easy, and being with her brought a sense of peace over him that he hadn't felt in years.

"What about your brothers? Where were they?"

"*They* were great. *I* refused to talk to any of them after the accident and they let me come to terms with everything on my own. Not one of them told me I'd be wasting my life by grieving."

"That's an awful thing to tell someone." After losing her parents, she would know. "Most folks are well-meaning. They try their best to provide comfort but sometimes it really is best for them just to be there and not try to offer up words of encouragement."

He let that thought sit for a minute. The accident had been brutal. The outpouring of support had been huge from folks in Gunner. Hell, one of the best things about being back without everyone recognizing him, was the fact no one looked at him with pity. They weren't being jerks. The emotion was genuine. He understood they were doing the best they could.

Had he been too hard on T.J.? Had Liam expected his father to have all the answers? Had he hoped and prayed his father would say something to plug the hole in his chest?

Was that fair to put on someone else?

"Now that I'm talking it through with you, I'm starting to realize that maybe my father did the best he could, too." Saying those words lifted more of the weight and brought a peek of light into a place that had been dark for so long. "My brothers did what they could, but they adopted the attitude that I'd talk about it when I was ready. I don't blame them because I know they acted out of love but maybe they should've pushed me a little more to talk about what happened. Because keeping all those feelings locked inside has been eating me up from the inside out."

The burst of air she sucked in made him realize she knew exactly what he was talking about and why he was sharing his story with her. And, no, he wouldn't push her to talk about what had happened to her. But she needed to know what holding it in did to a person.

Liam glanced around, his gaze locked onto someone. There was a young-ish looking guy in a hoodie who was emerging from a black sedan.

Savannah must've followed his gaze because she stiffened. "Does he seem out of place to you?"

"Yes. Don't turn around." Liam didn't live in Gunner anymore and hadn't in a long time. Some ranchers hired transient workers during calving season through the summer. So, this guy could be in town for legitimate reasons, checking out the park while he was there.

Liam walked Savannah off the concrete path and onto a bike trail, figuring it was the easiest way to tell if the creepy guy who now had on dark sunglasses was intent on following them. If this was a transient worker, Liam had the distinct advantage of knowing this area like the back of his hand. No amount of time could erase his memories of this place.

This area, this park had basically been his childhood and some of his best memories came from being outdoors underneath this wide-open sky.

"Is he following us?" He hated the shakiness in her voice even though she put up a brave front.

Liam wasn't ready to risk a glance backward or show his hand that they'd spotted the guy. He had another idea, but it would take her cooperation.

"Do you trust me?"

She looked into his eyes intently before saying, "Yes."

Liam liked the assured sound she made when she said that one word. More of that light peeked inside his chest and it had everything to do with Savannah. *Strange*, he thought, *considering they had barely just met.*

Being here with her felt like they'd known each other most of their lives.

"Good. This might sound like an odd request but there's a method to the madness. I'd like your permission to kiss you."

"Oh."

"It'll be easier for me to figure out what this guy's intensions are if he thinks we haven't noticed him. If he's a stalker, he'll think I'm your boyfriend and that should scare him off. If he's not, it'll give me a chance to watch him without drawing attention to the fact."

He turned to face her and saw that she was working her bottom lip pretty hard, scraping her top teeth over it repeatedly. The move shouldn't make him want to kiss her for real and not because it was the first idea that had popped into his mind. This was meant to be a ruse to ward off a creepy guy.

"We don't have to kiss. I could stand closer to you. Like this." Liam searched her eyes for a sign she was okay. Got one when she bit her bottom lip and gave a quick nod.

"We need to do something that gives the impression we're being intimate and like we're caught up in our own world. Is it okay if I put my hand here?" He motioned toward her waist not wanting to admit how many moments in the past half hour had felt just like that—intimate. Being at his favorite park and talking to Savannah was the best non-date he'd had in years.

She nodded quickly, and he wondered if her inability to speak was brought on by the sudden awareness that came with standing this close to each other. Heat ricochet between them. Stepping closer only intensified the electric sparks between them.

With those amber eyes staring into his, Liam almost lost focus. He looped his arms around her waist and was once again struck by the feeling of intimacy. Standing in the middle of a park on a bike trail shouldn't make the world feel reduced to the two of them.

It did.

BEING this close to Liam should have Savannah's nerves in a twitch. An odd thought struck her. She hadn't felt this comfortable alone with a man in more than a year, longer when she really thought about it. She could admit to being startled and maybe a little intrigued. Okay, maybe a lot intrigued. If she could feel this with Liam after only knowing him a short while, she could surely feel this with another person at some point in the future. *More baby steps*, she thought. And they felt good.

The fact her aunt knew Liam's family so well probably gave their afternoon a feeling of familiarity. Aunt Becky had known Liam for his entire life. Logic convinced her that was the reason that she felt like she'd known him longer than a few hours. Could it really only have been this morning that the two had met?

The progress lifted some of the heavy burden that had been docked on her chest for the past twelve months.

Savannah also realized that Liam was there with her instead of with his large family. Granted, he'd explained his complicated relationships, and boy did she understand that word more than she cared to admit. She thought about how much he'd shared with her right up until he stepped closer to her, looped his arms around her waist and made eye contact.

All logic flew out the window as her body instinctively leaned toward his masculine frame and she brought her arms up around his neck. The move caused her body to press against his. More of that electricity fizzled, humming through her body, searching for an outlet.

This close, the smell of spice and warmth enveloped her. She didn't realize how cool the air had been or how chilly she'd become until she stepped into his warmth.

And when his gaze locked onto hers, all she could think was how very much she wanted to push up on her tiptoes and kiss him.

8

Liam brought a hand up and brushed his thumb across Savannah's chin where it dimpled. Her breath hitched. And damned if her blood pressure didn't skyrocket. He saw her pulse beat wildly at the base of her throat. Her pupils dilated and all he could feel radiating from her was the unmistakable hum of desire.

It would be so easy to get distracted by her soft creamy skin, but Liam's protective instincts had kicked into high gear and he couldn't let his guard down while a potential stalker lurked around. He had to force himself to stay focused because being this close to Savannah had his mind snapping to other possibilities. And he had no business thinking of those under the circumstances.

The man was in Liam's peripheral vision. The hooded man was most definitely watching the two of them. He tucked earbuds in his ears and dropped down to tie his shoe. The dead giveaway that he was up to something was the fact both of his shoes were already tied.

Liam leaned closer toward Savannah to get a better look at the guy, and possibly a description. Her scent washed over him, another distraction he couldn't afford. Quietly, with his lips next to her ear, he whispered, "There's no reason to panic. I'm here. But I'm keeping my eye on him because he seems interested in us."

Savannah's muscles tensed, and the color drained from her wind-kissed cheeks. "What should we do?"

The urge to kiss her had to be forced from his thoughts. So, he dropped his left hand and took her right in his. "Let's walk. See what he decides to do. If he wanted to hurt one of us he could've already done so from inside his vehicle. So, we might as well figure out his intension. See how far he plans to take this."

"Is it safe to take a peek at him?"

The man's face was tilted toward his shoes so Liam nodded. "It should be okay if you're fast."

Savannah shot a quick glance. "It's not him. At least I don't think it is from here."

"Who?"

"The guy who makes me jump at my own shadow." Liam's assumption was confirmed about her past.

"Was he someone close to you?"

Savannah looked over Liam's shoulder, her gaze unfocused. "No."

Well, Liam really was confused now because the obvious answer to her skittishness was that she had an abusive ex. Or a date that had gone sideways. It was a sad fact that a woman's biggest threat was the man she should be able to trust the most, a boyfriend or spouse.

The trees behind Liam seemed to become suddenly very interesting to Savannah. When she spoke, her voice came out in whispered disbelief, "It can't be him. It's impossible."

"Why not, Savannah? Can't be whom?"

"Harley Patterson. Because he's under house arrest. He's constantly monitored." She said the last part so low he almost missed it. She glanced toward the man again. "This guy is the wrong size. Harley was much bigger."

Piecing together what little information Liam had so far, she must've known the man well enough to know his first and last name. His theory of a date going sour resurfaced. That, or someone else she knew like a neighbor or co-worker. He knew better than to push her for more information. He was patient and, besides, she seemed uncomfortable sharing this much. Trying to get her to open up would most likely have the opposite effect.

Savannah was as kind as she was beautiful. A twisted mind could confuse her gentle nature for her playing shy. Maybe even convince themselves she wanted them but pretended to be coy. Liam had grown up around enough law enforcement to have heard stories of men becoming fixated on women despite being rebutted. A shot of anger blasted through him and the fingers on his free hand flexed to ease some of the tension coursing through him. Liam refocused.

The man stood and started stretching his quads, then his hamstrings. He moved onto his calves as Liam squeezed her hand before leading her deeper onto the well-worn bike path.

This time when they moved, she practically plastered her side against his. When he lifted her hand, he noticed that her grip was so tight her knuckles had turned white.

"Are you okay?" he asked. "I can walk you to your car while I stay back and deal with this guy."

"The man I mentioned took so much away from me that night, not the least of which was my peace of mind." She took in a sharp breath. "I have to face my fear, or I'll never get it back. I'm tired of suspecting every person, thinking everyone I meet might hurt me." She stopped and chewed on her bottom lip again. "It's possible he's just a jogger. Right?"

"It is." While he'd showed interest in them for longer than Liam liked, the guy seemed to be getting into a running groove now. He'd gone through the same kind of warm-up ritual Liam had when he'd played sports in high school.

After a few tense minutes, it became clear he was doing his own thing on the trail. It could be an act. It was entirely possible the man had figured out that they'd spotted him. Either way, Liam wanted to get Savannah out of the park.

He glanced at his watch and was surprised to realize they'd talked for a solid hour back on the bench. Liam wasn't normally the chatty type. A good day for him meant he was up before the sun, barely exchanged a few words with his foreman, and spent the rest of the day alone on the land.

Talking to Savannah came naturally. It was as natural as the sun rising. And he found that he wanted to do more of it. But she looked tired and he didn't want to be selfish and keep her out when she had an early morning.

"I think it's safe to go to our cars now."

"Okay." He picked up on a hint of disappointment in her tone and damned if it wasn't a knife to the heart. His emotions were probably getting away from him because he was back in Gunner, facing down his past and not because the draw to Savannah was so strong he didn't want to leave her side.

She picked up their conversation thread, "I should probably go home anyway."

He guided them back onto the path, ever aware of the possibility that the man could still be lurking around. The ordeal seemed to have ruined her mood for going out to dinner.

Savannah was beautiful, warm and kind. He hoped she hadn't gotten herself into a relationship with the wrong man. One that had soured.

On the walk to their vehicles, she tightened her grip on his hand. She stopped before they reached her sedan. She shifted her weight from her right foot to her left and she looked at him like something weighed heavily on her mind.

"Thank you for telling me about what happened to you, Liam. That couldn't have been easy to talk about even after all these years." She blinked up at him with eyes that seemed able to look right through him. There was a connection there, too. One that said she might not know his exact pain but understood anyway. The broken parts in him connected with the broken parts in her. Together, they fit.

"I appreciate your willingness to listen." He deflected.

"I mean it. It takes a lot of courage to open up and talk about something so painful. If my opinion means anything, I just want to say I think you're incredibly brave. Stepping up to the plate to save someone else from shame and embarrassment, sacrificing your own happiness for someone else's makes you a hero in my book. It's easy to see what a caring person you are. I'm sorry you lost people you cared about so deeply."

He used the palm of his hand to rub his eye. "Looking back, I keep re-examining what happened that day. Wishing I could go back and change the outcome."

"It sounds like it was a freak accident and you're lucky to be alive. There was nothing you could've done differently, Liam."

He brought his free hand up to rest on her shoulder, using his thumb to trace her jawline. "I'm not the only one who is brave, Savannah. I don't know your past. If and when you're ready to talk more about it, I hope you'll trust me enough to tell me what happened to make you jump at every noise. Even if you don't, you're a survivor and you're putting your life back together. That makes you damn brave."

She smiled before she did the thing again where she scraped her teeth over her bottom lip. What was she working up to say?

With her free hand, she touched his arm. More of that heat radiated from contact. Her tongue darted across her lips, leaving a silky trail.

"Liam..." He had to lean in to hear her soft voice.

"What is it?"

"I have a question." Her cheeks flushed, and she looked even more beautiful if that was even possible. He had serious doubts it was.

"Ask anything, Savannah."

The question caught him off guard when she asked, "Will you kiss me?"

SAVANNAH STARED up into the most amazing pair of blue eyes. Black at the irises, surrounded by Caribbean blue waters. She could stand there and look into those eyes for days. After hearing his story, she realized why his eyes were so serious even when he smiled. Why his muscles seemed at attention even when he seemed like he tried to be nonchalant.

"Are you sure about that?" His voice was husky, and it was damn sexy. *He* was sexy as sin.

She pressed up to her tiptoes and nodded.

He brought his hands up to cup her face. Contact caused electrical impulses to fire through her. A jolt of awareness came with the nearness of his masculine presence. The scent of outdoors mixed with his spicy aftershave assaulted her.

But when his lips pressed to hers, his touch was so tender her heart squeezed.

Savannah brought her hands up to his chest as he deepened the kiss. She parted her lips and teased his tongue inside her mouth. Her breath quickened, matching the tempo of his. Another jolt of electricity rocketed through her. Awareness skittered across her skin, goose-bumping her flesh. She'd never felt so much heat and so much promise in one kiss.

He pulled back quickly—too quickly—and surveyed the area, reminding her how much danger they might be in.

"*Jesus,*" he whispered against her lips. The fact he seemed just as breathless and similarly affected caused warmth to pool, low in her belly, and need to well up.

Taking a second to breathe, she noted how right she felt this close to Liam. Being this close to another human, and especially a man, without a panic attack overwhelming her was progress. More baby steps. She liked baby steps. Baby steps were good.

Savannah made a mental note to call Detective Wade with Austin PD to check on Patterson's status. Last she'd checked Patterson was being monitored twenty-four/seven when her case had fallen apart because he wasn't properly Mirandized. The cops had been able to nab him on a lesser offense, which had won him a metal ankle bracelet. That knowledge allowed her to sleep at night.

Liam issued a sigh before a smile toyed at the corners of his lips. "I'll be around for the next few days at least. Let me give you my number in case you find yourself in a situation where you need a friend."

Savannah dug inside her purse for her cell and then handed it over. "Might be easier if you add yourself as a contact."

She noticed he had been keeping watch, even as they talked, and she appreciated someone having her back. She didn't need to be protected; she was fully capable of taking care of herself, despite moments of panic that were damn close to crippling at times. Point being...almost. She was a fighter and had kept fighting despite facing the scariest event of her life. She kept her head held high despite losing her friend in a cruel crime. And she was still there, fighting to regain her life. Losing sometimes, yes, but dammit, she needed to remind herself how much she'd accomplished in the past year.

She'd found a home in Gunner. Working at the bakery gave her a connection to family she'd thought long lost. It wouldn't be long before she'd be ready to get her own place again. Although, Aunt Becky seemed to enjoy having company and Savannah loved her aunt dearly.

The point was that Savannah didn't want to feel like she *had* to live with someone to sleep at night. Her job at the bakery was kind of perfect for her situation. She liked getting up at three a.m. and moving around when everyone else slept. She liked going to bed when it was still daylight. Black-out curtains were a godsend.

"Call any time. Day or night." Liam interrupted her thoughts.

"Be careful. I might just take you up on that, Liam."

His tongue darted across his bottom lip and more of that warmth pooled in places she'd neglected far too long. "I hope so."

He smiled a cocky grin that was endearing when her cheeks flamed at realizing the double meaning in her response.

"I didn't mean—"

"I know." He flashed straight white teeth. "But a guy can hope."

"See you at the bakery tomorrow morning?" She wasn't usually so forward, but what the hell? She liked Liam and there was no threat of anything serious happening between them, considering he was only in town for a short time. A voice in the back of her mind reminded her she'd learned more about him in the past few hours than people she'd known half of her life.

"I did have the best cup of coffee I've had in a long time this morning." He winked, and she appreciated the break in tension. God knew her life had had too much tension and not enough laughter. "The conversation was even better."

Her cheeks flushed at the compliment.

"I mean it, Savannah. I enjoyed talking to you this morning and this afternoon, which is saying a lot for a man who spends most of his days alone on a ranch and prefers it that way."

"Thank you. You're not so bad at conversation, either." Savannah hoped a good night's sleep could wipe away the worst parts of the day, and especially the part about needing her car to be pulled out of a ditch. As for Liam, he was the part of her day she wanted to hold onto.

"Then, I'll see you later." His deep timbre, combined with those words, sent a sensual shiver racing across her skin.

She climbed into the driver's seat before he closed her car door for her. She appreciated those little touches from him, that old chivalry that so many folks seemed to think was dead. And even though she could certainly close her own car door, she appreciated the gesture. Cowboy Code or just good old-fashioned Texas manners were timeless in her book.

He stood there, watching her leave while making certain no one seemed interested in her departure or followed her sedan.

There was more than chivalry that attracted her to Liam Quinn. It was probably just the fact that he was the first man she felt safe with in longer than she could recall that caused the strongest pull toward a man she'd ever experienced. But she was beginning to think it was a real shame he had no plans to stick around town.

9

The sun was descending into the western horizon. This was the closest to dark Savannah had seen in longer than she could remember, and the latest she'd come home in the past year. She was taking more of those baby steps and they felt good.

A voice inside her head said kissing a man she'd known less than a day was a helluva lot more than just baby steps. Under normal circumstances, she would agree, but nothing about Liam Quinn could be classified as typical. And, besides, just thinking about that kiss caused her cheeks to flame and set a dozen butterflies loose in her stomach.

"Hello," Savannah practically sang out as she walked into the entryway and then closed and locked the door behind her. There was no response from her aunt. Maybe she was in the shower and couldn't hear?

The two-story farmhouse's décor had gone untouched since Aunt Becky had bought the place lock, stock, and barrel before moving in twenty years ago. The entryway had a table for keys. The guestroom was off the entrance to her immediate right. The room was now occupied by Savannah. It had its own attached bathroom, which was incredible for this age of house.

A drawing room was situated to the left of the entryway and a hand-carved wooden staircase stood a little to her left. Positioned a few feet to the right of the stairwell, a hallway led to the back of the house. There was a large kitchen with a door that led to a screened-in porch.

Savannah listened for the sounds of water running upstairs but couldn't hear anything. She shouted her aunt's name again, and again there was no response.

That was strange. The front door had been locked and Aunt Becky's van was parked to the side of the house. She had to be home and she rarely spent time outside. She might be working in the kitchen and had earbuds on. Her aunt had made a big deal out of ordering a pair so she could 'blast' her music without interrupting her house guest.

Savannah tossed her handbag onto the chair in her bedroom. She took off her apron next. She was late for dinner and suddenly real-ized how hungry she was. Being with Liam had distracted her from a lot of things, not the least of which was food. Of course, she didn't mind being hungry now. Aunt Becky made the best lasagna and she'd promised to make a pan tonight. Based on the wonderful smells coming from the kitchen, she'd delivered.

"Aunt Becky. Are you home?" Savannah stood at the base of the stairwell, listening for a response. It was still a little early for bed, but Aunt Becky had said the bakery was hopping even more since Savan-nah's arrival in town.

A tinge of worry crept in. Savannah was probably overreacting, but she decided to follow her instincts and run upstairs. There was still no sound of water running in the shower.

Savannah couldn't wait to tell Aunt Becky about Liam. Or maybe she'd hold onto the details of their date. Because the kiss they'd shared was something special and a piece of her wanted to be selfish and hang onto it for as long as she could.

Liam was temporary in Gunner. He'd been clear about that. He had a career in Colorado. And she figured there was almost no risk in the kiss. Her heart wanted to put up an argument that everything about that kiss had been different. Special. Because not one kiss before it had burned with so much passion and promise. Not one kiss before the one tonight had made her feel lightheaded and lost in the moment in the best possible way. And not one kiss before had made her want so much more.

Liam Quinn had reminded her that she was still a woman. She had needs and desires that had been stuffed down so deep in the past year she thought they might be lost forever.

Having them resurface, knowing they existed had awakened part of her that was gone.

There was something lighter in her step, too.

"Aunt Becky?" Savannah stood at the top of the stairs. All the doors were open. If her aunt had been upstairs, she would've heard Savannah's shouting by now.

That creepy-crawly feeling pricked the hairs on the back of her neck again. The doom-and-gloom cloud descended around her and, again, her mind snapped to the worst-case scenario.

Savannah took the stairs two at a clip. She rounded the corner and made quick time rounding to the kitchen. Her aunt was nowhere to be found in the house.

It was too dark for her aunt to be in the barn and she didn't really like it in there anyway. She figured she better check anyway. Her aunt could've been hit with a bout of nostalgia. Savannah hadn't lived with the woman long enough to know all her habits, but in the weeks she'd been there so far, her aunt hadn't so much as darkened the door of the barn. Even the light was on a timer so she wouldn't have to make a trek out there to turn it off. Savannah could see the pain in her aunt's eyes when she talked about the loss of her husband. She could only imagine the pain losing a soulmate would cause.

After calling out a couple more times, Savannah headed toward the kitchen door. She double-checked her phone on the way, thinking maybe her aunt had texted or tried to call. Although she hadn't planned on going out for dinner with someone from town, Savannah supposed it could happen.

She didn't bother to turn the light on. The light outside the barn door was enough to light the trail from the house.

Stepping onto the porch, her foot caught on something and she tripped. She took a couple of steps forward to regain her balance, throwing her hands out in front of her to catch her if she hit the floor.

She rolled her ankle but caught herself on the wall. And then she looked down at what she'd tripped over, making out the frame of a woman. A flashback haunted her and she quickly reminded herself this woman wasn't Jenny.

Savannah stumbled toward the light switch. She hit the plate and finally found the switch, flipped it.

"*Aunt Becky.*"

Savannah's aunt was lying on her side, her right arm tucked underneath her body. Her lifeless body brought a flood of memories crashing into Savannah. She reminded herself to breathe. Aunt Becky needed help.

Dropping onto her knees, she felt around for her aunt's left wrist. She checked for a pulse. Relief flooded her when she got one. It was weak, but there.

Thank God. She'd take that miracle.

Savannah had dropped her phone in the tumble she'd taken. She looked around for it on hands and knees. Another wave of relief washed over her when she found it. She immediately called 911 and requested an ambulance.

Her next call was to Liam.

"What's wrong?" He must've realized she wouldn't call him tonight unless it was an emergency, especially considering they'd just parted ways.

"It's Aunt Becky. I got home and found her body on the back porch. She's breathing and has a pulse. An ambulance is on its way."

"Is she hurt or sick?"

"I have no idea." Savannah controlled the panic rising in her throat by slowing her breathing. She could do this. She *would* do this for Aunt Becky's sake.

"Is anyone else in the house?"

An icy chill ran up her spine at the implication. "No. I checked the house when I went looking for her after I got home. I didn't see anyone."

"Okay. I'm turning around and headed in your direction." She'd already heard his tires screech. "I'll stay on the line with you until the EMT arrives."

"Thank you, Liam."

"You said she's breathing."

"Yes. I checked her pulse. She's unconscious and it looks like she may have taken a fall." Or been knocked down. The realization slammed into Savannah that someone could've been in the house. Her mind snapped to the jogger from the park. He could've been a plant there to keep an eye on Savannah while his partner broke into Aunt Becky's house.

But for what?

There was no money kept in the house and Aunt Becky lived modestly.

"Is there anything around that you can use as a weapon?" Liam's voice broke into her train of thought.

"A knife." Savannah scrambled to her feet and ran into the kitchen. She pulled out the largest, sharpest knife from the block. She didn't think anyone was in the house, but he was right to warn her to be extra cautious. "I have a kitchen knife."

"Don't let your guard down until the ambulance arrives." Didn't that comment send another icy chill down her back. He was right, though. She'd be crazy to get too relaxed.

In the distance, she could hear sirens. "They're getting close."

"Good."

Savannah hopped to her feet and ran around the side of the house, ready to direct the first responders to her aunt. She stayed at the corner, so she could keep watch over the porch door and still see the ambulance as it arrived.

From across the street, she saw a male figure pacing on the large wraparound porch. Craig Whittaker?

What was he doing outside? Oh, right. Sirens. If she hadn't been the one to call 911, she'd most likely be on her aunt's porch trying to figure out which of their neighbors needed help, too.

Savannah made a mental note to circle back later and let him and his family know what had happened to Aunt Becky.

Siren off, lights still swirling, an ambulance roared up the drive and came to a halt. A female EMT, not much taller than Aunt Becky and much younger, came racing out of the passenger side of the vehicle. The driver was a few inches taller, male and solid muscle.

"Over here." Savannah waved her arms wildly. "It's my aunt. She must've fallen on the back porch. She isn't moving but she is breathing and she has a pulse."

"My name is Sheila Stillwater Raines. Your aunt's late husband was my uncle." The raven-haired woman hurried past Savannah, who shook off the momentary shock and followed.

All of a sudden, the feeling there was a whole world that Savannah was missing out on struck her, hard. She'd been so consumed learning the bakery business and getting her bearings since arriving in town that she hadn't even thought to ask if Aunt Becky's husband had relatives in and around Gunner.

She couldn't help but feel guilty and decided right then and there to rectify it once her aunt was better. And she *had* to get better. Aunt Becky *had* to be okay.

Cell phone still firmly in Savannah's hand, she picked up the pace behind Sheila. The female EMT and her male counterpart went to work immediately, dropping to either side of Aunt Becky.

"Does Aunt Becky have any known medical conditions?" The strangeness of hearing someone else call Savannah's aunt by Aunt Becky had to be shoved aside.

"None that I know of but that doesn't mean much. There hasn't been any reason for me to know her medical history and she seems as healthy as a wild horse."

"Is your aunt on any medications?" asked Sheila.

"I think so. I just moved in a couple of weeks ago and she joked about the handful of pills she takes to keep herself going. I think most of what she takes are vitamins, though. I can go get them."

"Pull me what you can from her medicine cabinet," Sheila directed as she checked Aunt Becky's vital signs.

Savannah bolted inside the house and up the stairs. She forgot all about the cell phone glued to her hand until she opened the medicine cabinet and saw the glint of metal.

Liam.

He'd ended the call.

She grabbed four bottles on the second shelf, which was all she could find among the travel-sized bottles of shampoo, floss and other sundries. Glucosamine and Vitamin D3 were the ones she recognized. The other two looked like legitimate prescriptions. She chided herself for not quizzing her aunt about medications before now.

Savannah didn't bother to close the medicine cabinet and she had no idea where she'd put the knife because the only thing in her hand was her cell. She made a quick scan of the sink for anything else that might be helpful and quickly decided nothing would.

With bottles in hand, she took the stairs two at a clip. On the second to last step, she lost her footing in her haste and the ankle that she'd rolled earlier screamed with pain. She took a hop-step but managed to stay upright and nearly careened into Liam.

"Thank God, you're here. The EMT asked for these." She nodded toward the bottles she cradled in her arm. "And I have no idea where I put a very large knife."

"About yay-big?" He faced his palms together about a foot apart.

"Yes."

"It's on the counter. I saw it a second ago." He steadied her by gripping her elbow, so she leaned some of her weight on his arm. He gave her a once-over, focusing on her leg. "What happened?"

"My ankle. I'll explain later. Right now, I have to get these to the porch so the EMT can evaluate Aunt Becky's medications."

Liam helped her as she hop-walked. The sight of her normally strong-willed and spunky aunt being loaded onto a gurney with an oxygen mask covering her mouth was enough to knock Savannah back a step.

A dark thought struck...did everyone connected to her have to die?

She recognized the irrational thought for what it was and shoved it aside. The possibility of losing Aunt Becky hit harder than Savannah expected.

The woman was strong and vital, Savannah reminded herself. Aunt Becky ran her own successful business and had for decades. She was a force to be reckoned with, far too lively to think anything bad could happen.

Savannah handed over the pill bottles to Shelia, her...what? Cousin by marriage?

The thought of having more family sparked an unexpected reaction in Savannah. It felt a lot like hope, an emotion she hadn't allowed herself to feel since losing her parents.

"Thank you." Sheila examined the labels and called out a few of the names into the radio clipped to a strap on her shoulder. She pulled a plastic baggie out of one of her pockets, tossed the bottles inside and secured the bag in a large pouch attached to the side of the gurney.

Through the haze in her mind, she heard terms like, *unconscious* and *female*. There were other medical terms used that she didn't understand and wouldn't have registered anyway.

When Sheila stopped talking into the radio, she focused on Savannah as her partner started wheeling the loaded gurney away. "We're taking Aunt Becky to Gunner General Hospital. You're welcome to ride in the front of the ambulance or bring your own vehicle."

"I can give her a ride." Liam stepped outside from the porch.

Sheila's eyes widened in recognition for a split second before she regained her focus. "Signs look good so far and I'm going to put her in the best hands possible. I'm sorry I haven't been by to meet you. Our aunt thought it would be best to give you some time to adjust."

"Are there more of you...us?" Savannah almost didn't know where to start.

"Afraid it's just me and you." She nodded toward the ambulance. "And our aunt."

Liam moved to Savannah's side as Sheila apologized and started backtracking.

"We'll be right behind you," Liam said.

Sheila nodded and waved. "We'll take good care of her."

Savannah was grateful for the ride because she wasn't sure how far she'd get with that rolled ankle. She could already feel it swelling as it pulsed with painful throbs.

"I can lock up if you give me a key." Liam helped her to the counter where she leaned some of her weight.

"It's in my purse, which I dropped on a chair in my bedroom when I first got home. My room is in the front hallway. You can't miss it." She couldn't help but wonder what else she didn't know about Aunt Becky's life.

Liam disappeared and returned a minute later, holding out her handbag. "You'll be able to find it faster than me."

She reached in, found the pocket, and produced the set quickly. "It's the gold one."

Liam locked up the screen door and turned off the porch light. He locked the kitchen door next. "We can lock the front on our way out." He glanced at her right ankle. "You'll need to ice that."

"I can ask for ice at the hospital. Staying here and not knowing how my aunt is doing is making me want to climb a wall."

"They'll take her back with the doctor and you most likely won't get to see her for a while." He frowned. "Is there anything you want to bring with you to the hospital? We have time to collect a few things now."

She was already shaking her head. "I'd rather get there and get settled in case she wakes up soon."

"Do you think we need to get my cousin involved?" She realized the implication as soon as he said the words. Bringing in the sheriff made this a criminal investigation.

"Not yet. I hope this is just an accident. She could've tripped and maybe hit her head. I didn't see any signs of blood, but it's possible I missed it. We won't know for sure until she wakes and can tell us what happened."

Savannah hoped there would be no need for law enforcement to get involved. She'd seen enough of the inside of a police station to last a lifetime.

10

L iam helped Savannah into his pickup before climbing into the driver's seat. He hightailed it onto the farm road headed toward the hospital, figuring he could get them there in less than half an hour without breaking too many traffic laws.

"My mind is spinning, taking me to a bad place. I need a distraction." Savannah stared out the front windshield. "Would you mind telling me more about you?"

"Let's see." He figured the lighter the topic, the better under the circumstances. Worry never solved a problem and he'd already seen tension lines bracketing Savannah's pink lips. Lips he'd thought about more than once since the kiss they'd shared in the park. "I graduated high school and attended University of Texas at Austin."

"Wait. I thought you followed your high school girlfriend to college. I didn't realize you'd gone, too." There was a lot they didn't know about each other.

"I only signed up for a semester before dropping out."

"Wait. How old are you?" she asked.

"Thirty-two." He glanced over in time to see her jaw drop. She seemed genuinely shocked and he remembered she'd told him she'd gone to the same school. But with an enrollment of fifty-thousand students in a town of close to a million residents, it wasn't a surprise they didn't know each other.

Still, it was a small world and they'd been running in similar circles for the better part of their lives and yet had never met.

"You do realize we're close enough to the same age to have been at UT together. What a crazy coincidence." She seemed to marvel at the odds.

Liam navigated onto the highway. "Considering we're both from Texas, both went to college and are reasonably smart individuals, the odds aren't all that bad that we'd both end up at UT."

"Well, that's a good point."

"I got a partial scholarship, went to class and worked part-time to help make ends meet. T.J. wanted me to work on the ranch after high school, so he cut me off financially. I'd bet money he expected me to come running home after a month in Austin. I decided to show him and got a part-time job."

"And yet you ended up working on a ranch anyway." She seemed to relax a little while they talked and he liked the fact her stress levels seemed to ease when she was with him. "What did you major in?"

"Sports." He chuckled at the irony of going to school for a sport he didn't care if he played. "Football, to be exact. I might've been good at it, but playing sports wasn't my priority. I accepted the coach's offer to get a break from my father, which was the same reason I played football in high school. If I wasn't home, my father couldn't put me to work. I guess you could say that was my big rebellion."

"Too bad your father missed out on having great sons."

"Have you met the others?"

"Not officially. Does one of your brothers have two little kids?"

"That would be Eli. He's the oldest."

"His kids are sweet. He brings them in sometimes on the weekends. They are two of the cutest squirts I think I've ever seen." She paused. "If any of your brothers are half the man you are, and your father doesn't see it, that's his loss as far as I'm concerned."

Liam wouldn't argue there. His brothers were amazing men and

T.J. was losing out big time. "Are you always this perceptive when it comes to people?"

Savannah cracked a smile. "It might've been mentioned before. I've always been a people watcher. People are so fascinating."

"And yet you keep most at a safe distance." Spending the late afternoon with Savannah had been right up there with one of his favorite despite the fact she'd been on edge for most of their time together. The kiss they'd shared had replayed in his head more times than he wanted to admit while on his way back to the inn. He'd barely started thinking about ordering pizza after he got to his room when the panicked call from Savannah had come in. And that voice —the undercurrent of terror had nearly ripped his heart out of his chest. He'd wanted to go all primal and protective even though Savannah was capable of handling herself.

"So, why can't I seem to do that with you?" The admission came out of the blue.

"If you figure out the answer to that question let me in on it. Because I've thought the same thing about you half a dozen times today." He chuckled but it was one hundred percent truth. "You know, I shut off my feelings toward T.J. a long time ago. Being home. Talking to you about my ghosts makes me wonder if he acted that way because he couldn't stand the pain of losing my mother. I'd blocked out all thoughts, good and bad, of my father. But, you know, I remember how much he seemed to love her. How he'd light up when she was in the room. Damn. I buried those memories along with my mother."

"Sometimes it feels easier to shut down, than deal with emotions. You were young and most likely thought you had to step up and be brave for your brothers. Kids have a way of blaming themselves during a loss. We take on so much responsibility for things outside our control." She stilled for a minute while he considered her senti-ment. It had sounded like it came from a place of experience.

Before he could respond, she continued, "I've been thinking about what you said earlier about opening up and talking about what happened in my past. The reason counselors couldn't help me had more to do with me than them. I closed up and haven't let anyone inside. I showed up for appointments and talked to them without telling them what was really bothering me. My real fears seemed so out of control that avoiding them felt like survival. I see now that I can't conquer my fears until I open up and talk about them."

"I'm glad you reached out tonight, Savannah." Gaining her trust was important to him for reasons he couldn't pinpoint. As it was, he'd been avoiding going home to the ranch. Although, a little voice in the back of his mind called him out. He'd *wanted* to spend time with Savannah today. He'd hadn't used her to avoid home.

But Liam would go home and he would face T.J., and then Liam would leave town.

A thought niggled at the back of his mind. If T.J. was sick...would he still want to leave?

From what he could tell so far from his conversation with Isaac, there were a lot of questions swirling around when it came to T.J.'s health. Liam could admit that he was curious about his father's news. Concerned? Yeah, he was that, too.

Of course, only four out of the seven brothers were currently in town. Liam had fallen out of contact with his family and had no idea what his brothers were up to other than Isaac. Hell, Liam was still trying to wrap his thoughts around his twin brother being married with a kid.

"Did you see any signs of a possible break-in at the house?" Savannah changed the subject and pulled Liam from his thoughts.

"Not at the doors. I could've swept the place and checked windows but didn't have time." Liam wanted to better understand what she was so afraid of.

"I keep wondering why my aunt would go out the back door. Thinking back, I've never seen her do that before."

"How much time do you spend at home together?"

She shrugged. "Awake? Not much." She had only recently moved in and the two spent most of their time bakery based on what she'd told him so far.

The hospital came into view. Savannah motioned toward the modern-looking white building. "We're here."

He gripped the steering wheel and navigated through the lot. After finding a space and then parking, he helped her out of the vehicle and into the entrance marked, ER.

Walking past the boxed-in waiting room with a room full of blue chairs and kids who were running around or crying, Liam helped Savannah to the registration desk.

"Becky Stillwater was brought in a few minutes ago by ambulance. This is her next-of-kin, Savannah Moore."

The intake nurse, a woman in her late-forties with frown lines creasing her forehead, nodded as she stared at the computer screen in front of her. She glanced up and then performed a double-take. She studied Liam's face.

"My name is Liam Quinn." He figured he might as well get it over with. She'd figure out he was a Quinn at some point.

Recognition of his last name dawned. She immediately stood. "We have another waiting room where you'll be more comfortable, Mr. Quinn. Let me show you and..."

The nurse seemed to be drawing a blank, so he helped her out, "Savannah Moore."

Liam didn't care for using his family name, but he didn't see a way around it after she recognized him. Considering a wing of the hospital was named in honor of his mother, thanks to a generous donation made by his father following her death, being incognito was out of the question. In this case, it would help Savannah. He was grateful to be able to do that.

"Please, follow me." The nurse came around the counter and badged them inside a restricted hallway.

Liam didn't do hospitals. Not after spending time in one as a patient after the accident. He'd been flown into Dallas's best trauma hospital. He'd been out of it the whole time and had no idea what was going on. Just being inside a place with white walls and white tile floors made him uncomfortable in his skin. Memories crashed down on him. First, of losing his mother and then of waking up to find he'd lost his wife and child.

The walls suddenly seemed to shrink, and he had to force air into his lungs. Even now, after seven years, the pain was so fresh, so real it felt like it had happened yesterday. The world tipped on its axis at remembering. And he'd stuffed so many of those recollections down there was no more room.

The nurse deposited them in a private waiting room. She stood at the door. "Coffee might not be fresh but it's strong."

"Thank you." Liam glanced at Savannah's ankle. "Can someone take a look at her? At the very least she has a sprain. Maybe worse."

"Of course, Mr. Quinn. It would be my pleasure." The nurse instructed Savannah to take a seat and, shoving his heavy thoughts aside, Liam helped her to the chair.

The nurse squatted down in front of Savannah. "My name is Kristin." She smiled. "Tell me what happened."

"I rolled it trying to get downstairs while retrieving my aunt's medicine for the EMT. It's probably nothing." Savannah tried to brush off the incident and the pain. Liam realized she wouldn't want to focus on herself at a time like this.

"On a scale of one to ten, what's your level of pain?"

"Honestly, I haven't been paying attention. It's not fun when I put weight on it. So, maybe a four." The way she'd winced when Liam had helped her to the chair made him think she was definitely down-playing her injury.

"She's having trouble walking on it without support," he added.

The nurse nodded. "I'll bring in the doctor."

"Oh, no. It's not that important." She tried to play it off but the nurse shot her a look.

"You're most likely going to be here for a while. It can't hurt to let the doctor stop by. In the meantime, I can wrap it for you to give it some compression. Ice should help with the pain. Is there anything else I can get?"

"Ice would be amazing. Thank you."

"I'll be right back." The nurse grabbed the armchair and pulled herself up to standing. A few strands of her mousy-brown hair fell out of her ponytail. She tucked the loose tendrils behind her ear and promised to be quick.

Before Kristin left, she looked at Liam. "Would you mind helping move one of these chairs so she can elevate her foot? She might be more comfortable that way and it will definitely help with swelling."

Liam obliged.

"Thank you," Kristin said before exiting the room.

Liam went straight for the coffee pot. He held it up to his nose, took a whiff and made a face when he was hit with the smell of hours-old coffee. "You want a cup of this?"

"Might as well give it a try." Savannah stared at Liam. "I'm sorry for being naïve, but it just occurred to me how much money your family must have to get this kind of special treatment."

It was Liam's turn to be embarrassed. "Sorry, I wanted to help with Ms. Becky and my father's name gets attention."

"But you're so down-to-earth." She sounded bewildered and it made him chuckle.

"My father has money. I, on the other hand, work as a ranch hand." He had the tan lines and rough hands to prove it.

"You could be doing nothing right now, and yet you chose to work at a hard job." Her eyes were huge.

"You're tired and overthinking it."

"Am I?" The tension on her face broke, replaced by weariness and exhaustion. "I'm exhausted but there's no way I could get any rest until I know Aunt Becky is going to be okay."

The waiting room had about a dozen chairs that looked like the kind he'd find at a small airport. There was a unisex bathroom and a sink with a coffee maker that came with all the fixings. He figured he'd better make himself comfortable for the wait.

"That's what this is for." Liam poured two cups and handed one over. "There's sweetener in case it's too strong."

Savannah blew on the hot liquid before taking a sip. "Wow. That'd bring a zombie back to life."

Liam couldn't argue there. "It's bad but strong. The nurse wasn't kidding."

Savannah twisted her face before taking another sip. "It gets the job done all right."

"If zombie waking is your thing. It delivers."

She smiled despite the circumstances and he liked being the one to put a smile on her face.

The nurse opened the door with her shoulder. Liam rushed to help because she had an armload of supplies, including two pillows.

"I grabbed one of these for your ankle and the other for your back." She fussed with making Savannah comfortable. Liam appreciated her for it.

"Thank you. That's much better."

The nurse dragged a chair around, positioning it so that she could work on Savannah's ankle. The woman was an angel. She made quick work of wrapping the bad ankle in a flexible bandage that looked like athletic tape.

"Your aunt is doing well. She's not conscious yet but there was a contusion to her head and that could explain her current state. It most likely happened when she fell. We have a wonderful staff of doctors here at Gunner General. Dr. Villanova is the attending and he's the best."

The reassurances brought Liam back to a dark time in his past—a time when everyone tried to convince him everything would magically work out.

Then, the shock and horror that came with being told his life would never be the same again.

11

"Does he have any idea what's wrong with her yet?"

The twinge of hope in Savannah's chest was cut short when the nurse shook her head. She did, however, place an ice wrap around the sore ankle and then secured it with an elastic strip.

Relief was instant.

"That feels so much better." Savannah bent forward and put her free hand on top of the ice wrap.

"It's probably nothing more than a sprain. Painful but not catastrophic. It's good to get the official blessing from a doctor just to make sure, though." The nurse stood and returned the chair she'd been sitting on to its previous location. "I'll see if there's an update on your aunt."

"Thank you." Savannah figured she wouldn't be getting this kind of special attention if she didn't have Liam Quinn by her side. It was strange to think he belonged to one of the wealthiest families in Texas, considering he was one of the most down-to-earth people she'd ever met.

As the nurse left the room, Savannah took a sip of her coffee, trying to gather her thoughts. "I need to make a few calls. Obviously, my aunt won't be able to open the bakery in the morning and I need to be here for her, so I can't make it in." She rubbed her neck, trying to break some of the tension that had been building over the past hour or so. Thinking about everything that needed to get done caused more of that stress to build. "I just need a minute to catch my breath and think this through."

Liam walked to the window and she realized his face had paled. She remembered what he'd told her about the accident that had taken away his family and she wondered if being in a hospital might be dredging up painful memories. Her heart squeezed at his loss. A stab of guilt nailed her because she'd been so busy worrying about her own situation that she hadn't considered what this might be doing to him.

"Why'd you stop talking?" he asked.

She shrugged. "I thought you might need a minute."

He blew out a sharp breath and his lips thinned as he stared out a dark window. "They are a big part of the reason I've been stalling going back to Quinnland. The accident happened on the property and I haven't been able to go back since then."

"I can't imagine your loss, Liam." The pain would be unimaginable. Savannah hadn't even been close to marriage with anyone she'd dated. Losing her parents had been devastating enough. The thought of losing a spouse and baby—and at such a young age—was unnatural. Her heart broke for him.

He tipped his chin.

Even though she could count the number of hours since she'd first met Liam, there was something about him that made her feel like they'd known each other all their lives. Two old souls? Two people who'd met in a past life? Savannah had no idea if that was even possible. All she knew was that she and Liam had a connection like none she'd ever experienced.

She thought about how much easier it was to talk to strangers sometimes. But this went beyond that. The two of them had opened up those wounded parts of their souls. Talking to each other felt like the most natural thing in the world.

She'd never experienced another connection like this, so she was swimming in new waters. And then there was the fact that electricity sizzled in the space between them when they were close to each other.

Liam studied the window and issued another sharp breath.

"Am I part of the reason you haven't gone home?" she asked.

He took his time responding with a nod and she wondered if he regretted helping her.

"Liam, don't think you have to stay with me if there's something else you need to do. If you want to go—"

"I'd rather you stop pushing me away." His words had a sharp edge. Is that what she'd been doing?

She could make an excuse or she could come clean. She decided on the latter. "I like being with you, Liam. But you should know that I can't allow myself to depend on anyone else."

"That's not true. I've seen it with your aunt." He made a good point. Had she been pushing him away, afraid he would just leave her anyway? It wasn't like he had plans to stay in town. And they'd only just met. How was it that she felt such a bond to him already that the idea of him leaving hit like a physical blow?

"You live in Colorado. You're visiting. I think it's easier to talk to you because there's no threat you'll stick around." She realized she'd probably hurt him when his jaw clenched.

"Being with you has been a welcome distraction, Savannah. I like you. A lot. Do I know exactly what that means? No. Between what's going on with your aunt and what I have to face at the ranch, this is probably the worst time to meet someone I could really care about. I didn't plan this and neither did you."

The part about caring so much in so little time rang true. The knowledge he would leave when his family business was settled hurt way more than it should at this stage.

"We barely know each other."

"Do you really believe that, Savannah?"

"Tell me how I'm wrong, Liam."

"I may not know all the little things about you like your favorite color or what you take in your coffee but those are just that...little things. Those things can be learned over time." He stalked over to her and cupped her cheeks in his hands. "I know that you're intelligent and have a kindness unmatched by most. I saw how you were with Sheila. You care about your family, even the ones you don't know that well yet."

She couldn't argue his points. He'd hit the nail on the head every time so far.

"Do you feel something different between us now? Something you've never felt with another soul?" This close, his spicy male scent washed over her and all she wanted to do was get lost in Liam.

She couldn't make eye contact because it would literally melt her right now. Instead of speaking, she nodded.

"Good. Because I haven't either. Who the hell knows what that means. All I know is that if we don't trust each other and take a few steps on faith, then whatever is happening between us dies right here. It'll never take flight."

The pull toward Liam was too much to ignore and almost too much to handle. The kiss they'd shared had been in another stratosphere. It had made her want. And she hadn't allowed herself to want anything in longer than she could remember. Because want that strong could only lead to disappointment. And it would crush her.

She wanted him to know why she held back. "Something happened last year that made me afraid of my own shadow. You've been around me long enough to realize that much, I'm sure."

He nodded.

"I'm a work in progress on overcoming it, because I refuse to live the rest of my life looking over my shoulder."

"Your fighting spirit is one of the many traits I admire about you." Well, damn. That statement could melt ice in the freezer.

Letting go and really feeling was more than she could handle right now. Plus, their situation was complicated, considering he lived in another state. If major life changes wouldn't need to happen for them to be together and slowly let this 'thing' play out, she might be more willing to open her heart. "This *thing*—whatever it is—that's happening between us needs to stay in the friendship zone. Because that's all I can handle right now, Liam."

"Look me in the eyes and tell me that's true, so I can believe you." His dare was met with a sigh.

She couldn't do it. She couldn't fake that she didn't want more. So, she didn't.

"Liam," she began, staring at the carpet.

"Up here, Savannah. I'm up here." It didn't help that every time she heard her name roll off his tongue the urge to lift her face toward his—the sun—and kiss him was a force all of its own.

"I'm not denying there's a strong attraction, Liam—"

"You've been fighting everyone and everything from the inside out for a solid year. I don't know what happened to you and you're not ready to tell me. All I ask is that you don't fight this. Let it be what it is, and let's see where it goes."

She knew if she looked at him in that moment, she'd cave. Deciding to be strong instead, she reached to undo the strap holding the ice to her ankle and then pushed up to standing.

"I'm sorry, Liam." Excusing herself to go to the bathroom might give her space she needed to think clearly. Because with Liam standing so close, those perfect lips of his within inches of hers, resisting the urge to tunnel her fingers in his thick hair and pull his glorious face toward hers to kiss him was getting more and more difficult.

Savannah cleared her throat.

"Excuse me," were the only two words she could muster.

In the bathroom, she splashed cold water on her face and then toweled off. It was so easy to get lost in Liam.

Fall down that slippery slope and she might never gain her footing.

A KNOCK SOUNDED at the door. Before Liam could respond, his father entered the room.

"Mind if I join you?" T.J. asked. With dark hair and blue eyes, there'd be no mistaking Liam for someone else's child. At six-foot-three, T.J. was a hair shorter than Liam, but the man was the same build of muscle. Isaac had joked their father always had a transparent king-of-the-hill attitude. He wore his usual outfit of jeans and a button-down shirt, his Stetson in his right hand.

"Suit yourself." Liam's guard was up. He had no idea what to expect with this out-of-the-blue visit. "Coffee could make a sloth run the hundred-yard dash in less than ten seconds. It doesn't taste good but it's strong. Do you want a cup?"

"Don't mind if I do."

Liam made a move toward the station, but T.J. brought a hand up.

"Stay where you are. I've got this." And then his father said something that nearly knocked Liam back a step. He asked, "Do you need a refill?"

"No, thanks. Mine's full." Liam had heard from Isaac that their father was acting differently. Seeing it with his own eyes was a whole different matter and caught him off guard more than he cared to admit.

"How'd you know to find me here?"

"Marianne's friend, Gert, works here. She called to check the house and make sure everyone was okay. At first, she swore she saw Isaac walk right past her in the hallway. Since he was standing in the same room when the call came in, I knew Gert wasn't talking about him." T.J. filled a cup slowly, his hand a little shaky. It couldn't possibly be from nerves, so the T.J.-being-sick theory jumped to the top of the list.

The door to the bathroom opened and Savannah walked out. She glanced up and stopped short. She performed a double take.

"My name is T.J. Quinn." Liam's father stuck his hand out.

Savannah took it with a smile. "Savannah Moore. It's a pleasure to meet you, sir."

T.J. practically beamed back at her. "Please, call me by my first name."

Well, that was another first. Even Liam's wife had been instructed to address his father as Mr. Quinn. It wasn't uncommon in Texas to show respect to elders in that way, but considering she'd become family, it was odd.

Liam reminded himself of the fact that a few little changes in his father didn't mean T.J. was a new man. That being said, Liam was curious.

"I hope I'm not being rude, but my ankle is still a little swollen and I need to sit down," Savannah said.

T.J. extended his arm before Liam could get to her. She took his father's offering and he helped her to her seat. She propped her foot on the pillow and repositioned the ice pack.

"Would you like to sit, T.J.?" Liam motioned toward a pair of chairs.

"Not unless you do." T.J. was tall by most standards and solidly built. When Liam really looked, he thought he detected a yellow-ish hue to his father's skin. His blue eyes weren't nearly as brilliant. It seemed like there had always been a twinkle in his father's eyes—a spark that was noticeably missing.

After getting a good look at T.J., Liam suspected his brothers might be onto something. Was T.J. sick? No one deserved to go through something like that alone. Not even a man like T.J. The man had been harsh and, granted, he'd been cold during Liam's childhood. People made mistakes. People changed. He'd seen it firsthand with Lynn.

T.J. had always been just as unbendable as steel. He'd been worse with Isaac who'd made a habit of drawing their father's ire to save the others from taking a beating, including Liam. No matter how much Liam had tried to stop his brother, Isaac had insisted. When Liam realized he was making things worse for his twin, he'd stopped.

Forgiving their father for what he'd done to Liam was easier than excusing him for his behavior toward Isaac.

Figuring his father wouldn't admit he needed rest even if it killed him, Liam took a seat. T.J. followed suit.

Savannah had turned toward her purse, retrieving her cell from it and, he imagined, doing her best to give them some privacy. He figured she was probably scheduling coverage for the bakery tomorrow morning.

The two of them needed to finish the conversation from earlier before they'd gotten distracted.

Liam locked onto T.J. "What brings you all the way down here, sir?"

12

"You haven't stopped by the ranch yet, son." T.J. held his hand up, palm out while he quickly added, "Which I'm not blaming you for. There are things between us that have been left unsaid for too long and I didn't want to miss a chance to speak up."

"I'm here in Gunner now. I showed up in town and I plan to make my way to the ranch." Liam's honesty was met with eyes that conveyed gratitude.

"You can't know how much I appreciate the effort you're making. You've done your part. It's my turn, Liam." T.J. stopped and if Liam didn't know his father any better, he'd say the man was getting choked up.

Surprise didn't begin to cover Liam's reaction to this entire visit. He took a sip of his coffee. He'd neglected the brew too long and it had gone cold. He probably should've taken T.J. up on the refill.

At least holding the cup gave him something to do with his hands.

"I've made a lot of mistakes in my life, son." T.J. paused a beat, looking like he needed a minute to regain his composure. "Losing your mother so young turned me into a terrible person. I did that. I got it in my head that life was unfair, and I let my anger fester. I closed myself off to everyone because I lost touch with what was really important. My family."

"It's understandable when you love someone." Liam threw his father a bone. The man was clearly struggling to maintain composure. And then there was the obvious comparison to Liam. Granted, not the same situation and not on the same scale but hadn't Liam done the same thing? He'd closed himself off from his brothers far too long. He'd avoided the ranch for years. Now that he really thought about it, he'd been unfair to those he loved. He hadn't seen the woman who raised him, Marianne, in years. It may have been her job to take care of the Quinn boys but she'd made it her life's work.

Damn.

T.J. leaned forward, resting his elbows on his thighs. "Seeing you go through the loss of a loved one nearly broke me in half. I gave the only advice I knew. Buck up. Move on. Pick up the pieces. It was a fool's instruction."

"We do the best we can under the circumstances."

"You lost your family, Liam. And there's no excusing how I treated you and your brothers." T.J. cleared his throat and tried to wipe away the moisture gathering in his eyes. "Your loss didn't make you hate the world. You only got angry at me and I deserved it."

"I was angry at the world for a good long while." Liam had to be honest with himself. He'd physically and emotionally shut down after losing Lynn and the baby. He'd pushed his family away.

"When you lost Lynn, I told you what I knew to do. What I'd done my whole life before meeting your mother. I'd always closed myself off to the world. Looking back, I can see it was defensive; if I didn't care about anything, I couldn't get hurt. Your mother changed that when I met her—I couldn't help but open up to her, love her. She made it easy. I'm sorry you never got to know her, but you boys remind me so much of her. She was the reason our marriage worked. I let her down by closing myself up after her death. And, even worse, I let you boys down. Seeing so much of her in the seven of you was too much."

"You were a single parent with seven kids. I'm sure you did the best you could." Liam didn't figure this was the time to point out how much they'd needed their father.

"It wasn't good enough, Liam. I should have been half the man you are, half the person your brothers turned out to be. She would've wanted me to take care of her boys because she loved each of you with everything she had. I failed her and I failed the seven of you, and I couldn't be sorrier."

There was so much Liam could say right then. He'd been angry for so long. And being angry never solved a damn thing.

In fact, it only made everything worse.

Liam never thought he'd see the day when his father offered an apology. The man's words seemed heartfelt, and yet it was next to impossible to erase all those years of hurt with a few words no matter how sincere they came across. Holding onto his anger toward his father had done little good for Liam, except to keep him in a state of frustration. He'd recently heard a saying that resonated right now, and it went something like, *Holding a grudge was like drinking poison and expecting the other person to die.* Liam didn't want his father to die —that wasn't the reason the quote came to mind—but he could see how holding a grudge against T.J. hurt Liam more than anything. And it had probably been a way to funnel all that unexpressed grief he'd felt. Besides, based on the tormented look on his father's face, T.J. had lived in his own hell for his shortcomings.

So, Liam did what he wasn't sure would ever be possible. "I forgive you, Pop."

"Pop," T.J. parroted. Those misty eyes gathered more moisture.

Liam leaned toward a shocked T.J., and brought him in for a hug. He hadn't called his father Pop since he was a young kid.

T.J. coughed into his bent elbow and said two words Liam had only heard his father use with hired hands and Marianne when they'd gone far above and beyond the call, "Thank you."

When Liam made eye contact with his father, he saw a tear break loose and run down the man's cheek.

"You can't know how much I appreciate this, son. I know I haven't earned the right, but I hope to gain your trust."

"I'm willing to give it a shot, Pop." At close range, Liam noted the bags under his father's eyes. The heavy circles. He couldn't help himself, everyone was wondering the same thing. "Is everything okay with you? You'd tell us right away if there was something to be concerned about. Right?"

"Big news is coming. It means a big change for me. But I'd like to have all my sons together to hear the news together under the same roof. Does that make sense?"

Liam couldn't be sure if his father meant because they would need each other for support or if he just didn't want anyone to feel left out.

"It does to me." Liam could see the changes in his father's disposition.

The door to the waiting room opened, interrupting the moment happening between them. A doctor entered the room, his gaze took in the occupants. His eyes widened when they landed on T.J. Liam mentally corrected himself...*Pop.*

"My name's Phil Newman. I'm Becky Stillwater's doctor." His gaze bounced from Savannah to Liam and then back to Pop. The doctor was in his mid- to late-sixties, had a bald head and wore round spectacles pushed back on his nose.

Liam bridged the distance between him and the doctor in a few quick strides and offered a handshake.

The doctor shook Liam's outstretched hand.

"My name's Liam Quinn. This is my father, T.J. Quinn." Recognition dawned in the doctor's eyes. "And this is Savannah Moore."

"Pleased to meet you all. And especially you, Mr. Quinn." The doctor's gaze locked onto Pop.

"The pleasure is mine." Pop shook the doctor's hand next. "Did you mention that you have an update on Becky Stillwater?"

Pop's inclination to get right to the point was appreciated under the circumstances.

"Yes, sir. I do. The good news is my patient is awake, alert, and talking."

It looked like Savannah took in a deep breath for the first time since the doctor entered the room. She didn't speak. At least not right away. She seemed eager to hear more about her aunt's condition.

"She suffered minor injuries. Her wrists are sprained from when she put her hands down to break her fall. This is not uncommon in cases like these with elderly patients," Dr. Newman said.

Savannah seemed a little startled when she heard the last words. With her aunt Becky's vitality, Liam figured that, like him, hearing her aunt being called elderly was a bit of a surprise.

"What happened to make her fall?" Savannah asked.

"Right now, she doesn't remember. She seems rather embarrassed by the fact. But again, that's not uncommon with patients her age. They slip, or they twist an ankle and end up going down. She hit her head on the way down. And that's the reason she's most likely experiencing short-term memory loss. However, that's something we want to keep her here to keep watch on overnight. Also, she hasn't had a physical in more than three years. So, we'd like to do a full workup."

"Absolutely, do whatever you need to do to figure out why this might've happened. My aunt is a very strong lady and has all her mental faculties. It must've been a fairly hard hit to the head to make her forget how she fell." There was something in Savannah's tone of voice that made Liam wonder if she thought the same thing he did. Maybe the fall wasn't an accident. Maybe someone was there for Savannah and when he realized he'd struck the wrong person, he bolted.

Liam figured he needed to check the house a little bit closer to make sure no one had found a way to break in. And he probably needed to get Griff out there at some point to double-check. Savannah had been resistant to the idea of bringing in law enforcement, so he'd be careful to explain his thought process.

"Then there's no reason she won't make a full recovery." Dr. Newman's gaze shifted from Liam to T.J. before refocusing on Savannah. "Running tests falls more on the precautionary side. But I think it's important."

"By all means."

Pop was already nodding his head in agreement. A thought

struck. Liam wondered if his father had been spending time with the doctor lately.

"Can I see my aunt tonight?" Savannah's back was ramrod straight. Liam knew her well enough to realize she wouldn't rest without seeing for herself that her aunt would be all right.

"Technically, visiting hours are over." The doctor had an annoying habit of glancing at Liam's father for approval before he spoke. "But in this case, we'll make an exception. Keep in mind, she needs her rest. And the best thing you can do for her tonight is go home and get some sleep yourself. She might need extra assistance when she's released from the hospital."

"Thank you, Doctor. I'll be sure to make all the necessary arrangements to take care of her at home once she's cleared to leave." Savannah's voice was all business now and Liam wondered how much that had to do with the doctor's insistence on skipping right over her to check for T.J.'s approval before speaking.

"I'll send a nurse by in a few minutes to pick you up and take you to your aunt's room." Dr. Newman turned to Liam's father. He started to speak but Pop shot a warning look.

What was that all about?

Savannah thanked the doctor one more time.

"Thank you, T.J." Savannah's comment was met with an arched brow.

"I'm not sure I did anything," came T.J.'s response.

"You being here helped more than you realize." Her gaze bounced from T.J. to Liam and back. "I'm pretty certain your presence is the only reason I'm getting to see Aunt Becky tonight."

Liam figured he'd seen just about everything there was to see until he noticed his father's face had turned red. Embarrassment?

"Like I said, I didn't do anything to deserve praise." He shot an apologetic look toward Liam. "But I'm glad my presence could help."

"Thanks for showing up, Pop. I mean it."

"That means a lot, Liam. And, once again," T.J. started, "if there's anything else I can do, and I mean anything, you just let me know. Your Aunt Becky is a dear person and a good friend of Marianne's;

it'd be my honor to help in any capacity I can." The sincerity in T.J.'s voice warmed more of the ice encasing Liam's heart toward his father. They'd made big strides tonight in their relationship. And maybe it was the fact that Liam had always rooted for an underdog that caused him to want his father to turn out to be genuine. "I'll leave the two of you now. It's late. I better get home to the ranch."

"It was really nice to meet you, T.J." With some effort, Savannah pushed up to standing. She embraced Liam's father. "I mean it when I say that I hope to see you again soon."

"Much obliged. I feel the same. I hope you come to the ranch with Liam for Sunday supper." T.J. shot a tentative look toward Liam. "That is, if you'd like to come back to Quinnland."

A knowing look passed between the two men, a new understanding.

As T.J. made a move toward the door, it opened. The nurse from earlier stuck her head inside the room and said, "I've been asked to take you to see your aunt now."

With a nod of his head, T.J. slipped out the door.

13

L iam held his arm out toward Savannah. She took it, leaning some of her weight on him.

"How's that ankle treating you?" Kristin asked.

"The ice is helping quite a bit actually." Savannah followed Kristin down the hallway, and to her aunt's room.

Inside, the lights were low. Savannah steeled her nerves by taking a deep breath. She wanted to have a happy face on for her aunt and had no idea what she would see when she walked into the room.

Much to her relief, Aunt Becky was sitting up and sipping on a straw. Savannah let go of Liam's arm and quickly made her way to her aunt's bedside.

"Sorry to have worried you." Aunt Becky's usual take-care-of-everyone-around-her attitude meant she was her normal self. Relief washed over Savannah.

"I'm just so happy that you're okay."

Aunt Becky studied Savannah for a long moment before speaking. "I honestly don't remember what happened." She shrugged like she was shrugging off any worry. "My foot must've caught on something and down I went. Flat as a pancake."

Her aunt's coloring looked good and the fact she was smiling broke the tension knots that had formed in Savannah's shoulder blades.

"Morning will come fast and you haven't changed out of your work clothes yet. As much as I'd love for you to stay, the business needs one of us up and running." It was just like Aunt Becky to put the business first, and it was another welcome sign that her aunt was feeling better. Though the thought of going home alone sent an icy chill racing down her back.

She cleared her throat and leveled her gaze, determined not to give in to the fear threatening to squeeze her chest so tight she could hardly take in a breath.

"I can open the bakery. No problem." Savannah figured she could catch a ride over after leaving the hospital, put her head on the desk and catch a few zzz's before it was time to open. She could freshen up in the employee bathroom, although at this stage a real shower and some clean clothes would be what dreams were made of. She could swing by the house and pick those up along with a toothbrush.

"I'm sorry for causing so much concern. I'm afraid I'm becoming a klutz these days."

"No apology needed." Savannah could only hope this was the result of an accident and not because she'd drawn someone dangerous to her aunt's home. A blow on the head could cause short-term memory loss. Savannah had read about it once.

"Go on and get some rest. The bakery's been extra busy since you joined me." Aunt Becky winked. She glanced up at Liam. "Thank you for taking care of my niece, Liam."

"I'm afraid I haven't done much except provide chauffeur services," he deflected. He'd been so much more than a driver and she needed to show him how much she appreciated him. Talk about a baptism of fire. Liam had been dunked straight in after their first meeting this morning.

"I'll stop by tomorrow to check on you." Savannah's promise was met with a genuine smile.

"Doesn't appear that I'm going anywhere tonight unless I can convince one of those male nurses to spring me." The older woman winked. At least her sense of humor was intact. All things considered, this was a good visit.

"Get well. It won't be the same at home without you there."

A hint of worry flashed behind her aunt's eyes. "I can call someone to stay with you."

"I've got this, Ms. Becky. That is, if it's okay with Savannah. I'd like to stick around and make myself useful. I'm not needed at the ranch right away and I'm rather enjoying spending time with your niece." Liam locked gazes with Savannah and she could tell that he was searching for a sign she approved.

She gave a slight nod, trying to stave off the flush rising up her neck that was heading toward her cheeks. Having his help had meant the world to her so far, so she tamped down her initial instinct to push him away. He'd asked her not to do that anymore. And, honestly, she was worn out from keeping the world at bay. It was time to relax a little and go with the flow as much as she was able.

Savannah pushed to her feet. Liam moved to her side and offered an arm. The knowing smile on her aunt's face caused more of that red heat to flush Savannah's cheeks. Ignoring it best as she could, she said, "Good night, Aunt Becky."

"See you tomorrow." Aunt Becky bit back a yawn.

The walk to the truck on her ankle proved trickier than Savannah had hoped.

"You sure you're going to be okay to work the bakery in a few hours?" Liam helped her inside the truck and waited for a response.

"I have to be. I called in extra help and I'll set a barstool in the middle of the kitchen and direct traffic if I have to." There was no way in hell she was letting Aunt Becky down after all the woman had done for her.

Liam settled into the driver's seat and within a few minutes, they were back on the road to the farmhouse.

Once arrived, she went straight into her bedroom and started gathering her things. She turned to Liam. "You asked about having your cousin out to check if someone might've slipped inside. It might be a good idea to double-check. I realize my aunt thinks she tripped but the thought occurred to me that someone might've struck her. I'm probably just being paranoid...but it would give much-needed peace of mind."

Liam pulled out his phone and fired off a text. "Done."

She thanked him.

"Does Bobby Raider come by often?" His arched brow combined with intense expression caused her to wonder if he liked Bobby.

"Every morning and he gives me the creeps. Why?"

"Every morning?" he parroted.

"Yes. I left the building yesterday, turned the corner and practically barreled into him. There's something about him that makes me uncomfortable." She flashed her eyes at Liam. "But then my judgment has been off lately when it comes to men. Everyone freaks me out except for you."

"I'll let Griff know to look into Bobby's whereabouts." Liam sent another text as she pulled out a gym bag and started stuffing it with her clothes.

"What are you doing?" He cocked his head to one side.

"I figured I'd grab a couple hours of sleep at the bakery then freshen up before we open."

"Why do that?" His cell buzzed. He checked the screen. "Griff can stop by in the morning. Said he'd prefer to investigate when it's light outside."

"Sounds good to me." She had no plans to be home anyway. "He can stop by the bakery and pick up the key."

"About that...how about staying at my place tonight." He put his hands up in surrender position. "I don't want you to get any ideas. It's convenient. Right next door. And would be better than sleeping on... what? A cot? Or—"

"Desk, actually." Her chest deflated a little at the fact he was so careful about making sure the suggestion wasn't sexual. She was attracted to Liam and he reminded her she was a woman. A woman who needed to feel normal again. And that meant dates and sex...and hold on a second. Was she saying she wanted to have sex with Liam?

A voice in the back of her head reminded her it was perfectly

normal to want sex again. It also marked a huge step forward in healing, because before him, she couldn't imagine herself alone in a room
with a man. This felt a whole lot bigger than baby steps.

"Does the fact that you're being quiet mean you're considering it?"
His voice was laced with hope and she knew he had the best of
intentions.

"It's a great idea, Liam. I'd love a few hours of real sleep." She
didn't mention the part about being alone with him was such a giant
step in getting her life back but the look on his face said he
understood.

"Good. I promise to behave." Again, her chest deflated a little at
how easy it seemed for him to shelve their attraction. She realized
how ridiculous it was for her to feel disappointed when he was
clearly just respecting what she'd said earlier. She could admit how
attracted she was to Liam. Hell, even her aunt seemed to have picked
up on the sexual current running between the two of them.

Savannah finished loading her overnight bag with supplies and
followed him back to the truck, careful to lock the door. On the
drive to his place, she leaned her seat back and grabbed a light nap.
When they arrived, he gently woke her and carried her bag to his
room.

"Shower's in there." He pointed to the adjacent bathroom. "Plenty
of towels. Knock yourself out."

A shower sounded like heaven and felt even better. Within twenty
minutes, she'd brushed her teeth and was dressed in her most
comfortable sleeping pants and T-shirt.

"Your turn." She stepped into the living room area of his suite.

His gaze swept over her, and her heart freefell. He gave a little
headshake before dropping his gaze to the carpet and walking right
past her.

When he emerged from the bathroom a few minutes later, shirtless and wearing jeans low on his hips, warmth pooled low in her
belly. She followed a drop of water as it trickled down a chest most
men could only ever dream of having. His body was straight off a
Times Square billboard.

"Didn't realize I was going to have company." He motioned toward his pants. "I normally sleep naked."

Her throat constricted at the thought of Liam in the bed next to her naked and glorious, male and masculine.

It was probably just the stress of the past few hours and the relief that Aunt Becky was going to be all right that was driving her to need to touch Liam. But boy did she ever need to touch him, and so instead of debating whether or not it was a good idea, she met him halfway across the room. She dug her fingers into his muscular shoulders to brace herself for the jolt of electricity that skittered through her every time Liam kissed her. Jesus, that man could kiss.

She closed her eyes and that's when the flashback assaulted her. She flinched. All her muscles went stiff.

Liam pulled back enough to hold up his hands with his palms toward her in the surrender position. He held one hand up for a few seconds longer like he needed a minute to catch his breath. It was a little too easily to get lost in the moment with Liam.

"I'm sorry."

"Don't be. Can you talk about what makes you jump every time I move?" He clenched his back teeth and she could see just how frustrated he was by her non-answers so far.

"Not right now."

"Then none of this is happening. I'm not that guy. I can't move forward with this, whatever this is, if I have to watch my every move for fear that I will dredge up a bad memory. But I have no problem waiting for you until you're ready, Savannah. Nothing needs to happen this red-hot minute."

"You would do that for me?" She blinked at him. She was pretty certain the man standing in front of her couldn't be real. She'd never been with someone who was so tuned in with her. She'd never been with another man who made her want to tell her secrets.

"You're worth the wait." He stabbed his fingers in his hair and smiled that crooked half-smile that made her want things. Things that were always outside her reach, like a real relationship with a man who made her knees feel like her bones were melting every time he touched her. As if that wasn't enough, he added, "And so am I."

Savannah blew out a frustrated breath. "Liam, you have no idea how much I want this to happen. I haven't been this close." She motioned with her finger between the two of them. "To a man in more than a year."

"You can talk to me, Savannah. You can tell me what happened."

"You have no idea how much I wish I could."

"Then do it. Talk to me. Trust me with what's going on." He locked onto her gaze and seemed to read the answer before she had a chance to speak it. "I'll still be here tomorrow. And the next day—"

"And for how long, Liam?" She wasn't mad at him so much as frustrated with the situation. She stared at him boldly and she saw in his eyes that he didn't have an answer for her.

"I'm here right now."

Savannah's back was against the metaphorical wall. Yes, she'd flinched. But, damn, she wanted Liam's hands on her more than she wanted air.

"He had me by the throat." She couldn't look in Liam's eyes when she spoke. "Just as I was about to pass out, the police came. They were about five minutes too late to save my roommate and friend, Jenny. But they saved me. He'd used a crowbar to jimmy the door open." It took a few minutes for Savannah to be able to breathe normally again. The panic in her chest caused it to tighten to the point she could barely take in air.

When she did finally look up at Liam, those pure blue eyes of his held so much compassion it caught her off guard.

"That shouldn't have happened." Liam's deep timbre washed over her and through her. This close, she could smell his unique woodsy aftershave. She'd memorized his scent. It was raw and spicy and male. All Liam. He said other words meant to soothe her. None of which could wash away the guilty feeling that always came with the memories of Jenny. Why Savannah? Why did she get to live and not Jenny?

Slowly, gently Liam brought his mouth to hers. He said against her lips, "You take the lead. You set the pace. If something makes you the slightest bit uncomfortable, you speak up. You can't hurt my feelings. And I want to make love to you. So, let's take our time; I've got all night."

Those words released a dozen butterflies in her stomach. She put her flat palms against the door to steady herself. She wanted, no, *needed* this.

"You are beautiful, Savannah." His pale blue eyes darkened with hunger. Just looking at him sent a thunderclap of need slamming into her.

Pushing up to her tiptoes, she pressed her lips to his. His tongue darted inside her mouth. He tasted like black coffee and peppermint.

Out of habit, Savannah closed her eyes. She immediately blinked them back open but didn't pull back. It felt good to be this close to Liam and she didn't want to break the moment. Words escaped her anyway. And as much as she appreciated how careful he was being, a piece of her wanted to let go with him.

So, she ran her fingers along the ridges of muscles in his shoulders. She dropped her hands to his chest, mapping him as she took in every glorious line before stopping at the scar tissue that ran from his collarbone to side rib. Her gaze shifted to meet his, and she held on for a long moment.

There was a flash of hurt in his eyes so intense and so powerful it almost knocked her back a step. Her heart pounded against her chest as need welled inside her. Liam was making it easy for her to let her guard down around him.

She crossed her arms in front of her and grabbed the hem of her T, pulling it up and over her head in one fluid motion.

"Jesus, Savannah. You're amazing." His gaze caressed her as tangibly as if it were his hands. "You're gorgeous. Can I touch you?"

Savannah took in a sharp breath and focused on how good it felt to stand this close to him and how much better it would be to have his hands on her. "Yes, Liam. I want you to touch me, and don't you dare stop."

14

"Tell me if I move too fast."

Liam searched her gaze as she gave a quick nod in response. He cupped her breast in his palm. Her nipple pebbled against the flat of his hand and his erection tightened.

He met her eyes, making sure she was okay. She slicked her tongue across her bottom lip leaving a silky trail and then brought her hands up to the snap of his jeans.

He covered her hands with his. "You should know before this goes any further that I don't do casual sex." He knew that the words were important, but it was taking every ounce of self-control that he could muster to move at this pace when he wanted to be inside Savannah more than he wanted air.

"Neither do I." Those beautiful amber eyes blinked up at him.

Making love to Savannah would change things between them. For the time being, Liam had no idea what that meant. He'd had his share of relationships since losing Lynn, none of which he'd exactly categorized as special in any way. But then, he hadn't been looking for special. He'd been looking for company. He'd been looking for companionship. He'd been looking for someone to make the long days and early mornings on the ranch where he worked in Colorado less monotonous.

A few of the women he dated over the years had said that he seemed distant. That he could never really connect. A couple more said they felt like they were competing with the ghost of his wife. The truth was that he wasn't looking for somebody he could love after losing Lynn.

In so many ways he blamed himself for her accident. The 'should haves' were staggering. He should have insisted she stay inside. He should have insisted she never climb on the back of that tractor. He should have kept her in Austin and away from the ranch.

But Liam was finally beginning to realize that he did deserve happiness, and if it came in the form of the beautiful and kind woman in front of him, then he'd do anything required to hold onto her.

And this was not the time to think about the past. The present— his future?—was right in front of him.

"As long as you're good with that." He dipped his head down and kissed her on the collarbone, feathering kisses at the base of her neck where her pulse pounded wildly. He smoothed his lips up the soft skin of her neck until he reached those gorgeous pink lips of hers.

Breathing her in, she smelled like spring flowers after the first rain.

So he leaned a little closer and kissed her. She parted her lips for him and teased his tongue inside her mouth.

Her hands went to the waistband of her pajama pants and he helped her take them off. As she stepped out of them he got a glimpse of silky purple panties. Liam groaned. Damn. He ran his index finger along the lace edging and she sucked in a breath.

Her soft curves and creamy skin nearly did him in. He needed to think of something else because being there with her while she wore nothing more than panties caused need to coil low inside him. Her long shiny hair cascaded down her back and his fingers itched to get lost in it.

Jesus, she was beautiful and he was just about the luckiest man in

Texas. The kind of connection he felt with her was not only the real deal, but he'd dated around enough to realize it was damn rare.

Savannah brought her hands to the snap of his jeans again. This time, he helped her take them off and then stepped over them on the floor. He searched her eyes for a sign that things were moving too fast for her, a look that would warn him to slow down.

When she smiled, his chest squeezed and he got the confirmation was looking for.

Anticipation already had his heart pounding his ribs. He flexed and released his fingers, reminding himself to take this very slow. He wanted to enjoy every last second.

"You're beautiful." His fingers grazed her shoulders and ran down the length of her arms. And then he trailed a line across her stomach, moving up until her generous breasts were in his palms. He brought his finger and thumb together to roll a nipple in between and felt her body tense. The little mewl of pleasure she released signaled he could move forward and the damn sound was so sexy it nearly did him in. He had to distract himself by thinking about anything but the sweet feel of her creamy skin under his rough hands and how much he wanted to be buried deep inside her.

Laundry. That was a much-needed distraction.

Liam hooked his fingers on either side of her hips securing her panties in his hands. He slid those down her soft curves. Laundry. His boxers joined her undergarments on the floor next.

"Kiss me, Liam." That was all the urging he needed to dip his head down and claim those gorgeous pink lips of hers. She took a step toward him closing the distance between them. Her body flush with his. He fisted his hands at his sides. She touched him first, bringing her hands up to his shoulders; her fingers dug into his skin as they deepened the kiss.

Laundry. Liam tried to distract himself thinking about the mundane task. Was it working? Not so much. And especially when her beautiful amber eyes opened and she looked directly into his.

To hell with laundry. Laundry could wait.

He leaned his head back enough to search her gaze. Before he could ask if she was okay, her hands dropped to his and then she lifted his to touch her body.

"I want to feel your hands on me, Liam. I've never wanted to feel a man's hands on me the way I want to feel yours right now. Touch me."

She smiled. The simple act caused an explosion in his chest of epic proportions. He was in deep. Not even thinking about laundry could save him now.

His erection strained to be buried deep inside her. He moved her to the bed as he kissed her so thoroughly they were both rendered breathless. Her fingers, quick and fiery, roamed his chest and arms. Got lost in his hair as she tugged and pulled, driving him to the brink of need.

When she brought up her legs and wrapped them around his midsection, he dipped his tip inside her. He swallowed her moan as she wriggled her hips until he reached deeper.

With a primal grunt, he buried himself inside her. She met each stroke with a movement of her own as need took over and they danced in a rhythm only the two of them seemed to know.

And then her muscles clenched around his erection as her fingers dug into his back. Her mewls strung together as she rocketed toward the edge and beyond. All he could hear was his name rolling off her tongue as she detonated around him. Allowing Savannah to set the pace, Liam surrendered to the need building inside him. Only then, did he give in to his own sweet release.

Gasping for air, she held onto him until the last spasm was drained from her body and she relaxed.

"Your body is the definition of perfection," he said in between breaths.

"No, but *yours* is. *You* are."

"What just happened was so much more than good sex. You know that, right?" He sure as hell hoped she did because this changed everything for him. He could be better about visiting home if he had a real reason to be here. A reason like Savannah. His mind already snapped to coming back to see her.

"It was okay." She laughed and her voice had a musical quality to it. He could get used to hearing it more often. When she smiled, it was like the sun was finally rising after weeks of rain. The dimple on her right cheek peeked out at him. He took it as a good sign. Savannah didn't smile often. When she did, damned if it didn't hit straight to his heart.

"Just okay, huh?"

"I'm not complaining." That bright smile lit up the room and he was getting to see a new side to her. One he liked very much and hoped to see more of. There'd been a rare few lighthearted moments between them. He'd let himself enjoy this one and give into the playful moment happening. He rolled onto his back.

"Hey, where'd you go?"

"I'm giving my ego a minute to recover."

"Oh, no. I was just teasing. I didn't mean—"

He held a hand up to stop her from taking him too seriously. His laugh started as a low rumble. He could get used to being like this, in bed, laughing, with her.

She laughed out loud this time as she repositioned until she curled in the nook of his arm. "I never exactly said it was bad."

"Nope. Worse. I think the word you used was *okay*." He feigned disgust.

"What's the matter, Mr. Quinn? Have you never heard that word before?"

"Not in the bedroom. Can't say that I have."

"Well, if I'm honest, the sex was a little better than okay." She pinched her finger and thumb together.

"No man wants to see that hand gesture while he's still naked."

That line really got her. She burst out laughing. And so did he.

"If I admit that was the best sex of my life—"

"Hold on right there. That's all you need to say," he teased.

The dimple peeked up at him.

"Fine. Then I won't finish, but it might've been a compliment that was even better."

"Not possible. You tell me I'm the best sex you've ever had while we're still in bed. Well, sweetheart, that's nothing but sexy. Game over. Stop there."

He had a feeling his heart shared the sentiment and he wasn't sure how to feel about that.

～

SAVANNAH SLEPT. For the first time in a little more than a year. She really slept. Like drool down the chin, out so hard she probably snored slept.

When she woke, the sun was out on a perfectly blue cloudless sky.

The clock read seven-twenty-six in the morning, which meant she was three hours late for work. "No. Shit. Shit. Shit."

She glanced around, looking for Liam. She heard noise coming from the other room and sat bolt upright. She glanced around and realized she was naked. She pulled the covers up to her chin as the door cracked open.

"Everything all right in here?" The door opened the rest of the way. Liam filled the door frame with his considerable size. Seeing him standing there calmed her rattled nerves.

"I'm late. I was supposed to be at the bakery hours ago."

"Your aunt called to check on you and said to let you sleep. She found cover for the bakery and wanted you to be free to meet with Griff this morning."

"What?" Savannah was pretty certain she hadn't heard right.

"She said not to worry about showing up until after the meeting. Said you haven't been sleeping and she was happy that you were. She told me not to disturb you."

"How did she know to call you?"

"She apparently tried your phone a few times before deciding to call me instead."

She must've given him a look because he said, "Don't worry. I told her you fell asleep on the couch and I didn't want to disturb you."

Her nerves calmed down another few notches. Her aunt had been nothing but kind, so it was important to Savannah to repay the kindness.

"You know she was young once, too." Liam leaned against the doorjamb and her heart faltered. "She seemed understanding. Actually, she seemed happy."

"That's because she worries about me too much." Savannah leaned back against the headboard and rubbed her temples.

"There's fresh coffee if you'd like a cup."

She made a move to get up.

"Stay right there. I'll get it." How she'd met a man as intelligent and sexy as Liam, she would never know. The fact he was about to bring her coffee in bed caused her to pinch herself. There was no way in hell she could be awake right now.

Liam Quinn was no dream. He was very much real as he handed her a fresh cup of what smelled like dark roast. And he was every bit the Adonis as he sat on the bed with his own cup in hand. Shirtless and with the kind of ripped muscles she'd expect to see in a magazine instead of real life, she thanked the stars for him being very much in front of her.

The coffee was as amazing as it smelled. "Thank you."

"For what? The best sex of your life or the coffee?" He smiled the devastating grin that launched a dozen butterflies in her chest and had been so good at seducing her last night. Damn. The thought struck she'd just spent the night with a man she'd known less than twenty-four hours. The thought caused her cheeks to flush.

"Both." She turned on the wattage right back at him.

"Do I get to ask what that was all about?" The sincerity in his gaze caused her stomach to do that flip-flop thing again, making her think a tiny Olympic gymnast had been unleashed inside her.

After what they'd shared last night she wanted to tell him something real. She blew out a sharp breath. "My aunt is worried because I can still hear her screams when I go to sleep at night. I can still see his dead eyes inches in front of my face when I close mine. People called me the lucky one for being alive. I'm not so sure it was luck."

Liam rocked his head and she could see how well he understood that statement.

"According to Detective Wade, Patterson got off on a technicality. The detective on the case was able to nail him for a felony. I checked in with Wade a couple of days ago and Patterson is still under house arrest and wearing the ankle bracelet. That was during my fifth move in ten months. And I haven't felt safe since, apart from the times when I'm with you."

Savannah waited for his response. She wasn't sure what to expect. Pity? God, she hoped not. She was so tired of people looking at her with apologetic eyes but not understanding what she'd been through in the least. They were well-meaning, don't get her wrong. She would never let them know how isolated she felt every time they looked at her with those sorrowful eyes.

When Liam looked at her, she didn't find pity. What she saw in his eyes melted her defenses. Compassion. A sense of comradery. Understanding.

"I'm sorry you lost someone you loved. That's the worst part in all this, isn't it?"

She was already nodding her head before he finished. "I felt so helpless. And then it was even worse when I saw her parents. I could barely look them in the eye. I should've been able to do more. Should have stopped him. I made a mistake when I let him see me. If I'd been a few seconds sooner, I keep asking myself if Jenny would be alive right now."

Liam was nodding his head. The rim of his coffee mug seemed suddenly very interesting to him. "Even though you did the best you could under the circumstances, I understand the feeling, the guilt, that comes with losing someone you love when you're so close to saving them. The 'should haves' that haunt you."

The fact that there was at least one other person in the world who understood what she was going through brought a sense of calm she hadn't felt in too long.

"Ever since I found out he was set free, I can't stop looking over my shoulder. You're the first person I've been able to let get this close to me without feeling like I want to jump out of my skin."

"Your trust means the world to me, Savannah." And then he made a promise she could only pray he could keep. "As long as I'm around, that bastard won't get anywhere near you."

15

Savannah believed Liam meant every word of that promise. But the reminder their relationship was temporary hit hard. The signs were literally all around her. The man was staying at an inn. It wasn't like he had a permanent home there in Gunner. Logic said that as soon as his business was over in town, he would go back to Colorado where he had a job and a home.

"What is it, Savannah? What did I say that was wrong?" He stood there, studying her and the way he looked so confused nearly melted her.

Should she tell him? She had no designs on him. They'd only known each other for a short while, although her heart wanted to argue the opposite was true. Time had no bearing on how well she knew someone. She'd known her Aunt Becky for her entire life and just found out that she had a cousin by marriage.

There was something deep and intimate in the connection she felt toward Liam and looking into his eyes right now, she convinced herself that he felt the same.

"I like you, Liam."

He smiled. "Why does that sound like you're about to tell me you don't want to see me anymore?"

"Believe me, that's the last thing you'd hear from me right now. In fact, I feel quite the opposite." She took a sip of coffee.

"That's a good thing from where I sit. So, why isn't it on your end?" He moved to the bed and sat on the edge.

"Because we live in different states, for one."

"That's just geography."

"It's a lot of miles, Liam. Some people would say we barely know each other." They certainly didn't know each other well enough to rearrange their lives.

Liam met her gaze and held onto it. "Is that really the way you feel? Like we're barely more than strangers? Because that's not how I feel at all. I already told you once that I would wait for you. I would wait until you were ready to take our relationship to the next level."

"That's true." No argument there.

"You telling me about what happened wouldn't have been possible for two people who didn't feel connected to each other." He paused like he was giving her time to argue. When she didn't, he continued, "I thought I knew Lynn. Hell, we grew up together. How could I have missed the signs we'd grown apart? I wasn't much more than a kid, but I've grown up since then and dated around enough to realize you and I have something special."

Everything he said made perfect sense to her.

"You and I might have only met a short while ago, but we know each other."

She couldn't argue this point. She felt the exact same way. She also felt a helluva lot scared by the fact. Maybe once she got her bearings again she could do this. Right now, thinking about him leaving in a few days made the air feel like it had been sucked out of the room.

Was this too much, too fast?

Her heart said no but logic said the opposite. She threw off the covers and hunted for her clean clothing. Gathering them up in her arms, she headed toward the bathroom.

"Where are you going?" The hurt in his voice almost stopped her.

Almost but not quite. She needed a little distance to get her head together.

"I have to go, Liam. I should go next door and work." Savannah quickly dressed and freshened up in the bathroom. Panic was settling in her chest and she needed to get out of there so she could breathe. "My aunt needs me to show up at some point and I don't want to let her down. I hope you understand. This whole thing...us...whatever that means is great but—"

He put his hand in the air in surrender, so she didn't finish her sentence.

Instead, she apologized and made a beeline for the door, noting that he followed her until she made it safely inside the bakery.

"Sorry I'm late, Ruby." Savannah greeted her aunt's friend as she entered the back room. She located an apron from the stock, and secured it. "I can take the counter."

"Hold on there a second, kiddo. You want to talk about whatever it was that put that tortured look on your face?"

"Not really." All she really wanted to do was get lost in her work and forget about all the confusing thoughts rolling around in her brain. Because those thoughts had her wanting more from Liam Quinn that she had a right to ask.

LIAM RETURNED TO HIS ROOM, confused. He glanced at the clock and decided to shelve his confusion for now. Griff had texted and Liam had just enough time to pull it together and meet him at the farmhouse. He grabbed his keys and wallet, and then headed out the door.

The drive to Becky Stillwater's house was quiet. Too quiet. It was odd because Liam usually liked quiet. The whole reason he worked a ranch was because he enjoyed his time alone.

Savannah was the reason for the change in him. He liked being with her more than he cared to admit. Being away from her felt like someone had punched a hole in his chest.

Griff's SUV was parked in the drive of Ms. Becky's house. His cousin rounded the side of the house as Liam parked. Griff was close in height to Liam. T.J.'s sons had dark hair while their cousins were more of the sandy-blond variety. Same chiseled jawline, or so they'd been told, usually following the calendar joke.

"It's good to see you, cousin." Griff embraced Liam as he exited his truck.

"You, too." Liam meant it. "It's been way too long."

Griff nodded his agreement. "Does that mean you're sticking around?"

"I'll let you know when I do." Liam chuckled. If Griff had asked that question two days ago, the answer would've been *Hell no*. Now, things had changed.

Griff didn't probe and Liam was grateful. He couldn't explain to another what he didn't have his own mind wrapped around.

"What have you discovered?" he asked.

"Follow me." He led Liam around the back of the house, stopping short of the porch. He pointed toward dirt. "The assumption so far has been that Ms. Becky was coming out the back door. But what if she was returning through it?"

"There are scuff marks here." Liam bent down to get a closer look. "Shouldn't there be footprints?"

"Yes, there should. Someone shuffled their feet to obscure the impressions." Griff moved toward the barn. "The line stops here at the grass." He looked up and Liam followed his gaze to the barn.

"Hold on a minute. What are you saying?"

"That Ms. Becky was trying to get back inside her house and away from someone when she fell." Griff held up his cell.

"Which would mean she found something she was trying to report."

"Her phone could've been inside the house."

"Maybe she followed a noise. Someone could've been here. Savannah has a past. Are you familiar with her story?"

"No."

Liam gave his cousin the high-level version, figuring he wasn't breaking her confidence. She wanted to find out what had happened to her aunt.

"So, what if someone came here looking for Savannah?" Liam started to pace. "Someone like Harley Patterson."

"I can run a check on the perp and make sure his ankle bracelet is still on."

"Okay. Say it was him. Why hit Ms. Becky on the head and then leave?"

"The perp could've confused the two women."

Liam slanted a look. "The two look nothing alike."

"Ms. Becky could've interrupted him or found him while he was casing out her home. He might've panicked and hit her on the head, which would indicate that she could've gotten a good look at him."

"That makes more sense," Liam admitted.

"We have to consider all the possibilities, Liam. This crime might not have anything to do with Savannah. She might have simply interrupted an attack on her aunt," Griff stated. "Or, the attacker was caught off guard and panicked."

"That doesn't make any sense. Wouldn't the person realize he or she would get caught when her aunt regained consciousness?"

"You're assuming the person has done this before or that she saw him well enough to identify him in a lineup." Griff stared at the barn. "The perp could be inexperienced. He or she might've panicked after knocking Ms. Becky out or assumed he or she had killed her."

He thought of Bobby Raider. "She doesn't remember anything leading up to the event. The possibilities are wide open."

Griff pulled out his cell and punched in a few numbers. He put the phone to his ear. "Hello, this is Sheriff Griff—"

Griff must've been cut off by the person on the other end of the line.

"Yes. Good to talk to you to," he said. Another beat passed. "Hey, could you do me a favor? Could you tell me who has been by to see Ms. Becky this morning?"

Another beat of silence.

"I see. She sounds quite popular." He rocked his head before making eye contact with Liam. Griff turned to face the barn. "I didn't realize she paid him to look after the barn. No, ma'am. That is nice of him to stop by and check on his employer."

More of that silence.

"Thank you for the information, Stella. You've been most helpful." Stella Barnes was one of the most social widowers in Gunner. She'd met and married the love of her life, who'd passed away before hitting sixty-years-old. Stella never married again. She'd said no one else would measure up to her Harry, so she didn't see the point. She didn't come across as lonely, either. Liam thought he truly understood the sentiment after spending time with Savannah. When the right one came along, there was no question.

Griff ended the call and motioned for Liam to follow. The two of them made quick strides toward the white barn.

The place was large enough to house three stalls, a wash room, and a tack room big enough for a desk to be pushed up against the back wall near the window. The building had high ceilings with exposed beams.

There was a light, airy feel to the barn. Nothing seemed out of place. Except maybe it was too clean?

Liam's family kept their barn immaculate and it wasn't *this* clean. Granted, no horses had lived there in a few years. Even so…

"Do you smell that?" Griff asked, moving toward the middle stall.

"Is that bleach?" There shouldn't be any use for bleach in a barn. Granted, some folks might say it could be watered down and used to kill insects, but T.J. had always said he never knew how the chemical might react with others in the barn. Also, bleach mixed with urine could create a dangerous gas.

"Do you see anything out of the ordinary?" Griff asked.

"No. In fact, everything's perfectly in order." Liam moved around the barn, checking for signs of mischief. He had no idea what he was looking for. Drugs? Weapons? Signs of a stalker?

"Too in order?" Griff wrinkled his nose as he moved through the space, walking into each stall and checking their corners.

The pungent smell hit even harder near the wash room.

Griff must've noticed, too. He locked eyes with Liam. "It's time to have a conversation with Craig Whittaker."

"Do you know the kid?"

"He's eighteen. Hardly a kid. Rumor has it he's been looked at by a few FSB Division One coaches."

"I can tell Savannah doesn't like him." He skipped the part about her being suspicious of men in general, figuring Griff would pick up on it.

"Since he lives across the street, we might as well stop by and ask a few questions."

"Can't hurt." Liam followed his cousin across the road to the Whittaker place.

A truck and a small SUV were parked on the pad next to the house. The two-story farmhouse could use a coat of paint. There was a broken-down sofa on the porch and a few empty beer cans stacked on a side table that had three legs.

Liam took in the scene.

"Craig Whittaker's stepdad returned not long ago. I'd heard rumors the two didn't see eye-to-eye." Griff's voice was low as they took the couple of steps to the porch.

Liam remembered that Savannah had mentioned that Craig Whittaker came from a broken home. Liam recalled something about a no-good stepfather who'd returned, making Craig's life difficult.

Griff opened the screen door and knocked.

There was noise on the other side of the door. Obviously, someone was home. That same someone didn't seem real interested in talking to the law.

Griff knocked again, louder this time.

Then came the hushed voices.

16

G riff knocked a third time. "This is Sheriff Griffin Quinn. Is anyone home?"

Liam's hands were already fisted at his sides as he took a step back and scanned the area. He took note of his cousin's hand that was now resting on the butt of the gun in his side holster.

A vehicle pulled up across the street. Liam watched as Savannah stepped out of the passenger side. She stopped and surveyed the vehicles parked at her aunt's house before she turned around and put her hand over her eyes to block the sun.

There was no way he could leave Griff alone on the porch, so he pulled out his cell and texted Savannah to stay put, wondering why she'd come home in the middle of the morning. After the way she'd rushed out, part of him hoped she'd come to clear the air.

The sedan drove off and Savannah moved toward the front porch, taking a seat on the steps. A return text came back with a thumbs-up symbol.

The front door opened a crack.

"Is your son home, Mrs. Hurler?" Griff asked.

The woman shook her head, but it was too late. Savannah

jumped to her feet and pointed to the left of the house. A text came, *Craig just ran out from behind the house.*

Liam showed Griff the screen, who spun on his heel, hopped off the porch and headed east. He radioed in the fact he was in pursuit of Craig Whittaker, who was wanted for questioning in Becky Stillwater's attack.

Racing toward the thicket, the younger man had enough of a head start that it would be almost impossible to catch him once he made it to the tree line. And he was almost there.

Liam cursed. He needed to tell Savannah to get inside the house. With phone still in hand, he managed to tap on her name a second before he followed Griff into the mesquites. Zig-zagging left and right, branches slapped him in the face.

Savannah answered but what he mostly heard was static. She said something he couldn't make out because her voice cut in and out.

"Go in the house and lock the doors," he said into the phone. "Stay away from the barn."

The call dropped.

Liam had lost sight of Craig.

"Do you see him?" he asked Griff.

"Thought I did."

The sound of an engine cranking in the distance cut through the air. Craig must've had a dirt bike stashed in the woods. Not exactly the actions of an innocent person.

"Dammit," Griff said. "He's getting away."

Liam tried to call Savannah.

No cell connection.

SAVANNAH STARED at the cell in her hand, trying to make out what Liam tried to tell her. His words were choppy due to a bad connection. All she heard clearly was the word *barn.*

She pushed off the porch and rounded the house. The barn door was open. She figured Griff and Liam must've been there and he must want her to find something inside.

The smell of bleach assaulted her the minute she stepped inside. Everything was tidy. Although she hadn't stepped inside a barn before, this one seemed exceptionally clean. What could Liam have possibly wanted her to find?

Savannah tried to reach him again but the call went straight into voicemail. It figured. The minute she really needed her phone to work so she could reach out to someone, it wouldn't. Cell coverage was spotty in this area. Liam would most likely call back when he hit an area with service.

As she waited for his call, she walked through the place. The bleach smell was enough to knock her out, so she decided to make her way back to the house. The creepy-crawly feeling that someone could be watching her had returned and she wanted to get inside and lock the door.

Nearing the barn door, it started to slide closed.

"Hey." She bolted toward it as her pulse skyrocketed. Before it completely shut, Craig Whitaker slipped inside.

Savannah froze. She heard a whoosh sound in her ears because she stared into eyes as black as Harley Patterson's had been.

"Where do you think you're going?" Craig's voice had a note of excitement mixed with pure hate.

"I'm right here. I'm not going anywhere." She managed to take a few steps backward, walking slowly so she wouldn't trigger a chase response.

"You messed up my plans and now you have to pay for it." His gaze narrowed, a lion zeroing in on a gazelle.

"My name is Savannah Moore and you don't know me. There's no way I could've—"

"Stop," he shouted. "Just stop it. Everything's ruined. They'll find everything out and it's your fault."

Craig stalked toward her and Savannah's freeze response kicked in. He grabbed her by the neck and backed her against a beam. The back of her head banged against the solid wood. His fingers closed around her neck, putting too much pressure on her windpipe.

Savannah gasped. Panic washed over her.

And then anger struck like lightning through a blue sky.

She pulled from all her strength as his grip tightened, drawing her right knee up to connect with his groin.

His face morphed, and he ground his back teeth, but his grip was relentless.

"Not. This. Time." Savannah raised her hands to his face and dug her fingers into his eye sockets.

He took a step back and knocked her sideways in the process. She flew through the air and then landed hard on the brick.

She scrambled to her feet and bolted toward the tack room. Craig was right behind her as she pulled anything she could get her hands on and chunked it toward him, a bridle, a saddle.

Her hand landed on a hoof pick as Craig got a fistful of her shirt. He yanked her backward, challenging her balance. She lost her footing but nailed him in the face with the metal end of the hoof pick.

"Bitch." Blood squirted from his forehead as she scooted away from him and toward the closed door.

She'd never get there in time to open it before he grabbed her again, and he was right behind her. All he had to do was reach up and grab her. And he would.

So, she dropped down and then curled into a ball.

He stumbled, tripping over her and landing hard on the other side. This put him in between her and the door. Savannah cursed.

Craig's black eyes shifted from the door and then back to her. He let out a laugh. "What do you plan to do now, sweetheart?"

"Kick your ass." Savannah threw herself at him. She white-knuckled the hoof pick and drilled it into his face.

He spit blood and looked at her with a shit-eating grin. His meaty hands closed around her shoulders like a vise grip.

Savannah didn't hear the barn door open. But she did hear the words, "Put your hands where I can see 'em or I'll shoot you dead right now."

Griff's voice caused Craig to lose focus enough for her to twist away from him. He kicked at her and connected with her right shoulder. It hurt like hell but the cavalry had arrived.

A second later, she heard a grunt and all she could see was Liam dive-bombing into Craig.

Griff stood over them, weapon drawn and aimed at Craig's head. "Give me a reason to shoot, you sonofabitch."

Craig grunted as Liam spun him around, face to bricks. With his knee jammed into Craig's back, Liam said, "He's ready to be cuffed now."

Savannah sank onto the bricks and gave herself a moment to breathe.

The next thing she knew, Liam was at her side, helping her up.

"Jesus, I couldn't reach you. He must've circled back. He had a dirt bike stashed in the thicket. He'd been planning this all along." Liam threw a kick, connecting with the stunned football player's thigh as he was forced to sitting.

"I want a lawyer." The arrogant jerk spit more blood.

Griff read Craig his rights before he walked him out of the barn and stuffed him inside the back of his SUV.

"Windows are cracked. He isn't going anywhere." Griff used the key fob to lock the door as a deputy pulled up. With his window down, Griff shouted, "Stay here and make sure he stays put."

The deputy nodded.

"Let's get you sitting down," Liam said to Savannah. He offered an arm and she took it. He walked her to the bench on the front porch and helped her ease onto it. "We can make a run to the hospital to see your aunt and get you checked out in the process."

"I need to know why he did this to Aunt Becky and to me. Griff might find answers. I want to stay." And she wanted Liam to stay with her. She looked up at him with pleading eyes.

"Fine." His concern was appreciated.

Adrenaline was starting to fade and the pain in her ankle was real.

Liam leaned toward her and she wrapped her arms around him. He pressed his forehead against hers and seemed like he was trying to catch his breath. "I didn't think we'd get to you in time, Savannah. I can't lose you."

"I'm here, Liam." And she hoped he meant those words because she felt the exact same way about him when he'd taken off to chase a killer. The thought of never seeing him again nearly crushed her.

Liam pulled back enough to look into her eyes. "He looked like hell by the time we got there. You did good, Savannah."

Despite the intense moment, she couldn't help but smile. With blood all over his face, she'd done a number on Craig. And she was damn proud of how she'd fought back.

"No one makes me afraid of my own shadow again. I want my life back. Only better this time." She searched his eyes. "I want my life to include you."

LIAM LOOKED into the eyes of the woman he loved. Loved?

Hell, yes. He loved Savannah.

He'd strapped onto that roller coaster ride the minute he laid eyes on her at the bakery. She was smart, kind, beautiful. It went without saying that she was sexy. The moments when her sense of humor shown were some of his favorites.

Was she still scared? Yes. Hell, so was he. Being in a real relationship meant putting his heart on the line again.

But there was no going back now.

Liam looked at the woman who'd stolen his heart. *Really* looked. He'd known it the first time, but he was even more certain of it now. He'd found home.

"A man would be an idiot to let a woman he loved get away from him." Granted, he and Savannah hadn't known each other for a lifetime. They hadn't grown up in the same town even though their families had a connection.

None of it mattered. He'd been married to someone he'd known since childhood, who'd shocked him by cheating.

Liam had known he was in trouble since the bakery. He'd known, down deep, that he'd met *the one*.

Life could be random. Time was a thief. And as far as Liam was concerned, when a man found true happiness he should grab onto it with both hands and never let go.

Besides, the relationships he'd seen succeed were based on trust, communication and honesty. They worked because two people fell in love and decided to stay together for the rest of their lives. There was nothing magic about making a marriage work. Being together, staying together was a choice. And he chose Savannah.

So, he took her hand in his and dipped down onto one knee. Suddenly, he was as nervous as a teenager asking for a first date.

"Savannah Moore. I love you. I have never met anyone like you and I'm damn certain I never will again. We haven't known each other for long, but that doesn't mean what I feel in my heart and know in my soul is off base. I don't need to know you for a lifetime to know that you're honest, kind, smart, and beautiful. I don't need to know you for a lifetime to know that no one has ever made me feel as out of control in the best way possible. And I don't need to know you for a lifetime to know I'll never stop loving you."

His gaze never wavered from her when he asked the question that had been on his mind. "Will you do me the incredible honor of becoming my wife?"

Savannah smiled the kind of smile that could melt a glacier.

"I love you, Liam. Everything in my life has brought me to this point, to be right here with you. Life can take away everyone who is precious to us. I've never loved another person the way I love you. I never will love another person the way I love you. And I can't think of a bigger honor than to live out the rest of my life with you as your wife."

Liam looped his arms around his future bride. Her body, flush with his, fit him in all the perfect and right ways. He dipped his head down to claim her mouth.

He didn't know how long he kissed his bride-to-be. He stopped when he heard Griff clear his throat in the background.

"What did you find out?" Liam asked as he helped Savannah to her feet. He looped one arm around her waist, allowing her to lean some of her weight on him. He knew full well that she could take care of herself, but he liked the thought of being strong for her when she needed it.

"His mother cooperated when I threatened her with obstructing justice charges by lying to us when we knocked. She let me in his room, which she admitted she was never allowed to go inside. Turns out, this guy has been researching how to get away with murder. Ms. Becky was most likely going to be his first victim. I found a small collection of bleached bones in his room. He's been killing animals to get a feel for what it will be like." Griff's face morphed in pure disgust. He shifted his gaze to Savannah. "You interrupted his plans, so it seems he planned to get rid of you first."

She recoiled a little but then her chin jutted out in defiance.

"Guess he's had a change of plans."

"He turned eighteen last month. There shouldn't be any reason for him not to be tried as an adult. A judge won't like seeing any of this evidence with a person this age."

"Sounds like it will only get worse."

Griff nodded. "I'm heading to county lockup to get this guy processed and behind bars where he belongs. A couple of my deputies will finish processing the scene."

One of the deputies had already gone to work, but all Liam could think about was being there for Savannah.

"Thank you, Griff. For everything," she said.

"Take care of him for me." Griff motioned toward Liam.

Savannah smiled. "Already planned on it."

"Don't be a stranger in town," Griff said to Liam.

Liam smiled and nodded. He wasn't ready to share his plans to stick around with anyone but Savannah just yet. They had some figuring out to do before sharing their news.

"Swing by to give an official statement when you're ready."

Savannah said she would before Griff disappeared into the driver's seat of his SUV and then backed out of the drive by going around Liam's truck.

"Can I stay with you at the inn?" Savannah asked.

"I can do better than that."

She looked up at him. Confusion knitted her brows.

"Do you trust me?"

"I better if I'm about to be your wife."

"Good point." He walked her to his truck and helped her into the passenger side. "I have something to show you."

THE HOUSE WAS JUST as Liam remembered. Big. Beautiful. He drove down the lane and parked to the side of Casa Grande. He had a home on the property that he was ready to claim.

"Do I get to know where we are?" Savannah asked.

"Home."

17

EPILOGUE

In or out. Make a decision, Quinn.

The engine in Phoenix's pickup idled as he sat in front of Casa Grande. He rested his hand on the gear shift. His fingers flexed. With a flick of his wrist he could back out of the parking spot, turn around and drive home to Austin. He could ignore his father's request to come home and quash his interest in the announcement.

A crush of memories assaulted him. This place had meant more to him than just a work camp. Although it had been just that during his childhood. Hell, he credited his father for giving him a relentless work ethic as a result. Thoughts of running through those fields with his brothers, tossing a football around or cracking jokes made the ranch feel like home.

Being the youngest of seven, Phoenix had watched four of his older brothers move away the minute they could. The two who'd stuck around had been lifelines even though he rarely saw them during his high school years. By the start of senior year, he'd kept a running countdown of the days until it was his turn to move on.

Phoenix had left Quinnland in the rearview the day after graduation and had never looked back.

Fast forward seven years and there he was, debating his next actions.

Four of his brothers waited inside the house. The twins, Isaac and Liam, had recently returned to Gunner at their father's request and seemed to have found true love. Isaac had gained a beautiful step-daughter in the process. Liam had sounded the happiest Phoenix had ever heard him on the phone yesterday. Noah and Eli still lived and worked on the ranch.

His brothers weren't the reason he sat there listening to the hum of his engine instead of parking his truck, getting out of the driver's seat and walking inside.

Taking in a sharp breath, Phoenix cut off his engine and palmed his keys. He opened the door and stepped out of his pickup.

The only reason he'd made it this far was his love for his brothers. The chance to see four of them under one roof had been too good to pass up. He'd hoped the other two would show but no one had been able to reach Cayden. His number had changed, and he had yet to touch base with anyone in the family. Not a huge surprise considering he was one of the best tracker-for-hires in the state. Poaching was getting more and more sophisticated. The criminals seemed to be getting harder, too. And even though Cayden was the best at his job, the work was becoming more and more dangerous every year. Phoenix hoped to get word on their brother during this trip.

Lastly, his brother, Aiden, had sent Phoenix a text with three simple letters after receiving the request to come home, WTF. Phoenix's thoughts exactly. Why should any of them bother rushing home at the request of a man they didn't know or respect?

Phoenix took his time walking to the door, half expecting it to fly open and Marianne to come running out. She always called when she came to Austin and he always went out of his way to meet up with her. Marianne was gold. T.J. Quinn was a whole different story.

The reason no one had heard him pull up was evident the minute he opened the door. He heard lively chatter coming from the kitchen in the back of the house. He'd committed to making an entrance, so he forced himself to keep going by following the sounds of his brothers' voices.

He took off his Stetson and set it on the table in the hallway and then walked into the kitchen. Talking stopped. Four of his brothers, three of his newly-minted sisters-in-law and three kiddos in highchairs sat around the table. Gina's mother was at the table, as was Ms. Becky from the bakery. Sheila Stillwater sat next to her. And then there was T.J., who surprisingly sat on the side like the other adults rather than the helm.

Marianne, who'd been standing at the island, turned around when the noise-level stopped.

"Phoenix." The word came out of her mouth in a shriek.

He shot a smile at her as she padded over and wrapped him in an embrace. He hugged her and smiled when she took a step back looking pleased as punch.

"Take a seat, son." T.J.'s words caused a painful stab between his shoulder blades. His father had lost the right to use the word, *son*, when he'd denied them his love all those years ago.

Standing there, looking at a family he should recognize as his but didn't caused his blood to boil for reasons he couldn't pinpoint. This was exactly what he'd wished for as a little kid. So, why did everything inside him want to revolt against it now?

Was it too little, too late?

He'd driven a long way, so the idea of turning around and walking out the front door shouldn't be crossing his mind right now.

And yet, there it was. He skimmed the faces at the table. Thought about the easy laughter he'd heard a few minutes ago. He'd never felt more like an outsider at Casa Grande. An odd feeling settled over him and the urge to get fresh air was so strong he couldn't ignore it.

"I can't do this. I can't pretend to be something we're not." Phoenix got out of the house so fast he forgot his favorite hat.

On his way out, he heard three words from his father, *Let him go.*

To continue reading Phoenix and Kaylee's story, click here.

ALSO BY BARB HAN

Don't Mess With Texas Cowboys

Texas Cowboy Justice

Texas Cowboy's Honor

Texas Cowboy Daddy

Texas Cowboy's Baby

Texas Cowboy's Bride

Texas Cowboy's Family

Cowboys of Cattle Cove

Cowboy Reckoning

Cowboy Cover-up

Cowboy Retribution

Cowboy Judgment

Cowboy Conspiracy

Cowboy Rescue

Cowboy Target

Crisis: Cattle Barge

Sudden Setup

Endangered Heiress

Texas Grit

Kidnapped at Christmas

Murder and Mistletoe

Bulletproof Christmas

For more of Barb's books, visit www.BarbHan.com.

ABOUT THE AUTHOR

Barb Han is a USA TODAY and Publisher's Weekly Bestselling Author. Reviewers have called her books "heartfelt" and "exciting."

Barb lives in Texas--her true north--with her adventurous family, a poodle mix and a spunky rescue who is often referred to as a hot mess. She is the proud owner of too many books (if there is such a thing). When not writing, she can be found exploring Manhattan, on a mountain either hiking or skiing depending on the season, or swimming in her own backyard.

Made in United States
North Haven, CT
16 March 2022

17171718R00088